REIGN OF FOUR

BARANOVA BRATVA
BOOK TWO

MISTI WILDS

Reign of Four

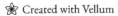 Created with Vellum

Contents

AUTHOR'S NOTE

Reign of Four is a direct sequel to book one of the Baranova Bratva, *Rule of Three.* If you have not read book one, STOP RIGHT HERE. I mean it. There are *huge* spoilers ahead.

Reign of Four is also darker than *Rule of Three.* Please check content warnings on my website prior to reading.
MistiWilds.com

If you're ready, turn the page.
Valentina isn't the only one who needs a little revenge.

Chapter 1

Valentina

If I close my eyes, I can almost smell the sweet perfume of roses. See their soft, scarlet petals trailing across the floor. Feel the touch of a lover across my skin, from tender presses of lips across my shoulders to reverent brushes of fingertips sliding down my waist, like ghosts whispering their love one breath at a time, lulling me into a comfortable sleep.

If I keep my eyes closed a moment longer, I can continue the game of pretend. I can tell myself that the coarse rope binding my wrists behind my back isn't real, that the copper tang in the air is a trick of the mind, that the ache behind my eyes is from staying up all night, consumed by love, instead of burning with hatred. That I can wake up any moment, and none of the pain tearing through my heart or body is real.

But the harsh grind of a metal door scraping against a concrete floor can't be mistaken for anything else. The way my captor's footsteps thud down the hall, a hum in the air as he *happily* returns to his most precious prize, can't be erased. The frantic beat of my heart, fluttering against my ribs like a caged bird, can't be wished away.

Reality wraps its icy arms around me in an embrace that squeezes so tight, it suffocates.

I can't play pretend, no matter how much I want to. I can't sit here and do *nothing*. I can't say I love my men and let my psycho ex-boyfriend *win*.

I have no doubt that my men are looking for me right this very second. Andrei will be barking orders to everyone within earshot, ensuring that not a single moment is wasted. Mikhail will be combing security feeds and spending thousands by the second to increase the Bratva's surveillance parameters. Ezra will be scouring the earth for any trace of me, hunting me down with every tool at his disposal, legal or otherwise.

It's not a matter of if they will find me, but *when*.

I need to ensure I survive until then.

I need to ensure I survive *in one piece*.

A shiver runs down my spine as my captor draws near. If you had asked me six months ago, I would have told you that Liam West, my ex-boyfriend-slash-boss, was harmless. Love-struck, sure, but average in every other facet. Not a threat. Not violent or sadistic or covetous. He was, in my mind, as normal as any businessman could be.

But the memory of the needle, the ache in the muscle and the bruise across my neck, remain as reminders of his true nature. The drugs in my system may have worn off by now, but the memory of my kidnapping never will.

Liam West is a fucking *traitor*. A *stalker*. A man obsessed with binding me to him, stealing me away from my intended to claim me as his. But he's too late. My heart and body already belong to three other men—three men who will tear Liam to shreds for everything he's done . . . and has yet to do.

By the time Liam shoulders open my prison door, I'm ready for him. He hums appreciatively as the door screams shut behind him. "If I'd known you'd look this good tied up, *zhena*, I would have suggested it years ago."

As he scans my body from head to toe, a ripple of delight in his eyes, bile rises to the back of my throat. I have no doubt I look as ragged as I feel, from the ache in my limbs to the scratch in my throat and all the other nicks and cuts along my skin. My beautiful wedding gown that Celia custom designed lay in shreds across my shoulders, pieces of the bodice and skirt torn off in the struggle to relocate me from the chapel to this dungeon.

I fought Liam every step of the way until he sucker punched me in the gut and knocked me out cold.

The fucking bastard.

I wish I had some of Ezra's skills to get out of these ropes and strangle the motherfucker with them.

The past few times he's come to check on me, he's been empty-handed, save his sinister smile. This time, he bears a tripod tucked under his arm and a tablet clutched in one of his hands. With a smile, Liam crosses the distance between us and plants a kiss on the top of my head. "Be a good girl, and maybe we can see about untying these, hm?" He fingers the rope that cuts across my chest and ties me to the cold metal chair. "Let you sleep in a bed tonight instead of that chair." He cups my chin and tilts my head back, forcing me to meet his eyes. "Don't you want to share your husband's bed tonight, Valentina?" His fingertip traces the seam of my lips, brushing against the gag shoved between them.

If he hooks that finger between my teeth to remove the gag, I'll bite the damn thing off.

A silent moment passes between us as he gazes down at me. Then, without another word, he gets to work. Humming happily to himself, he sets up the tripod and tablet across from me, flipping it so that the screen faces me. After angling it just right and tapping the screen, he smiles broadly as the front-facing camera clicks on. I catch my ragged appearance and clench my eyes shut.

I hope no one ever sees me like this.

"Perfect. Now all we have to do is wait." Liam steps behind me and wraps his arms around my shoulders, leaning in and burying his nose in my hair. He breathes deep, a shudder rolling through him as he catches a whiff of my conditioner. "Vanilla and honey," he groans, sucking in a breath. "Your favorite."

It's not, and as much as I want to laugh at him for misremembering, a shard of ice slices deep inside my heart as my mom's face flashes to mind. *She* loved vanilla and honey, not me.

I hope she isn't looking down at me from Heaven. I don't want her to see this.

I hear footsteps and two men talking, their voices carrying as though far away. The room Liam and I are in is silent, and as far as I know, it's only us in this place . . . wherever that is. I screw my eyes shut and try to remember where Liam took me after our wedding ceremony, but it's all a blur of blindfolds and sharp turns from the back of a moving vehicle, until he gut-punched me.

I have no clue where we are.

Dread settles heavy in my gut, but hope cuts through it just as quickly as I remember who the fuck my boyfriends are.

Ezra's a jack-of-all-bloody-trades, part bodyguard, part tracker, part enforcer. If anyone can find me, it's him. With Mikhail's money and Andrei's influence within the Bratva backing him, nothing will stop them from finding me.

A voice cuts through the tablet speaker. "It is empty. She is not here."

My heart drops.

Ezra.

"Well, *someone's* been here, or there wouldn't be blood all over the fucking hardwood." Mikhail's voice pitches as he lets out a frustrated yell. "Where the *fuck* did that *suka* take her?"

I'm right here, I want to scream. *Come find me. I'm here.*

"Take out frustration on enemy, Mikhail," Ezra chastises, his voice louder than before. They must be walking closer to the microphone. Is Liam playing a recording from earlier in the day, or are we spying on them live?

"Wait—what the fuck is that?" Footsteps, then a growl, loud enough that it reverberates through the room. "*Ezra.* Get over here."

Liam takes a breath and presses a kiss to my cheek. "Smile for the camera, *zhena.*" With a tug, he unties the knot holding my gag in place and removes it from my mouth, dropping the soiled cloth to my lap. "We have an audience."

My heart slams harder against my ribs, wanting to flee Liam's side and return to my men's. I stare at the screen and wait for my men to appear. All I see is a tiny picture of me and Liam in the corner. The rest of the image is black.

Paper rustles through the speaker, and the image on the screen lightens from black to white as something shifts on their side. Mikhail's face fades into view, his warm amber eyes cutting into my soul as our gazes meet through the video feed. A wave of Russian flows past his lips, too fast for me to catch what he's saying.

The image blurs and Ezra's face replaces Mikhail's. The audio crackles as he exhales hard.

"That *bastard.* I'm gonna cut him up into little, tiny pieces and feed him to the *fucking* rats. Do you hear me, *mudak*? I'm fucking coming for you." Mikhail's anger roars like thunder, sending fresh tears to my eyes.

"Mikhail—" My voice cracks. I swallow, but it doesn't do shit when your throat is dry as fuck. I try again. "Ezra—"

Liam cuts me off before I can get any other words out. "Isn't she beautiful, boys?" He caresses my cheek while my two lovers glare at him through the screen. "I thought you might want one last look."

"*Fuck* you—"

"*Mikhail.*" Ezra sighs. "What do you want, Liam? Money? Women? We will give all in exchange for Valentina." His expression remains passive, but his eyes burn with contained fury, sparking like embers in the night sky.

I have no doubt he's lying. All of my men will tear Liam limb from limb before they give him anything, after what he's done.

Liam hums idly, like he's considering Ezra's question. "What I want?" His grip on my cheek tightens, his fingers digging into my flesh. I flinch as the inside of my cheek presses painfully against my teeth. "Why, I have everything I want right here." He leans down and presses a quick kiss to my lips. As our eyes meet, his shoulders tense and a darkness fills his gaze. "But now that you mention it, perhaps there *is* one other thing I want, since you're both here." Releasing my cheek, he slides his hand into his pocket and pulls out a switchblade. With a flick of his wrist, the blade slides free from the handle and glints in the light. "I seem to recall one of you having a fondness for knives."

Panic ripples across my skin. Mikhail stabbed Liam in the shoulder the night Liam assaulted me in the alley. Then, he gave me that very same knife to hold while Ezra carried me back inside the club, all four of us leaving Liam to his own devices as he lay bloodied and bruised on the dirty concrete.

I stopped my men from killing Liam because I didn't want to watch him die. I didn't want to watch him suffer.

Now, I might pay for that kindness.

Liam pretends to study the blade, scraping the pad of his thumb against its edge. He pulls his finger back, and a bright red line forms as his blood quickly pools around a shallow cut. "It would be a shame if my hand slipped."

Ezra growls. "Do not touch her—"

Liam's eyes flash dangerously, and he bares his teeth at the camera. "She is *mine*. I'll touch her whenever I fucking please." He rubs his bloodied thumb against my cheek, visibly streaking my skin red. The copper tang of his blood fills my nose, and I hold my breath and clench my eyes shut to keep my stomach from churning.

If I keep my eyes closed, I can play pretend—

"If you don't believe me, I'll have to prove it to you."

My eyes snap open just in time to catch a glimpse of my men's fury as Liam swoops in for a brutal kiss, locking our lips together in a grandiose display of affection. He grips my shoulder tight with his bloodied hand, no doubt leaving another smear of red, like he's marking his territory.

A whimper catches in my throat, and he smiles against my lips, no doubt having heard the sound. I pray my men didn't hear it.

When he finally pulls back, he shoves my face away from his, a dark laugh passing his lips. "See, boys? Mine to touch all I want." His gaze flicks lower, and dread seizes my spine.

"Don't," I breathe, my voice barely a whisper. "*Please.*" The last thing I want is for Mikhail and Ezra to witness my shame as Liam forces himself on me. I meet my ex's eyes and plead for the part of him that might actually care for me to hear me now, to stop this before it's too late.

If that part of him still exists, it doesn't listen.

"Hold still, *zhena,* or I'll nick that pretty skin of yours." Liam flicks the blade against my shoulder, cutting my dress strap free. It falls limp, and Liam drags the flat edge of the blade across my chest on his way to cutting the other one free. He pauses then, like he expected my dress to fall from my body from gravity alone, his eyes narrowing like it offends him. With a scowl, he taps the sharp edge of his knife to the dip in the sweetheart neckline, pricking my skin with the tip of the blade. I flinch, and his eyes flick up to my face. "Don't move, baby, or what happens is your fault."

I suck in my cheeks and bite down on both sides, hoping the pain will ground me enough not to move. I glance away from Liam to see the screen. Ezra's face is missing, but Mikhail's is right there. His anger morphs before my eyes, turning softer once tears pool in my eyes. "Count your tears for me, love, and I'll make the bastard pay for each and every one, I *promise.*"

As Liam grabs the top edge of my bodice and starts carving through the fabric, it's Mikhail's voice that keeps me sane. He murmurs things to me, gentle things, but I can't make out the words over the sound of my dress tearing. Liam's knife isn't sharp enough for a clean cut, so he saws through the fabric, fighting for each inch. Fire licks at my skin where the knife cuts into my flesh, and my tears finally start to fall as, inch by inch, Liam tears away my defenses.

I count each and every tear, as instructed, committing the number to memory.

Once Liam reaches the skirt, he steps back to admire his work. Without the bodice holding me in, my breasts spill free, barely contained by the scraps of fabric left. My skin stings where the knife made contact, each shallow breath I take burning in my lungs.

Liam runs his palm down my naked flesh, from my sternum to my abdomen, across the fresh lacerations. My entire body flinches hard as I try to move away from the source of my pain. He notices and clicks his tongue. "Come now, *zhena*, it's your fault you're injured, not mine."

What?

Blood roars in my ears loud enough that it drowns out Mikhail's own outburst of rage. "I'm not the one holding the knife," I hiss, glaring up at Liam. Every nick on my body stings, but the cuts aren't deep. They're merely surface wounds, *thank God*, but that doesn't make any of this better. It sure as hell doesn't make it my fault, either.

Liam's eyes meet mine, his smile feral. "Would you like to be?" He holds the knife out in front of my face. The tiniest bit of red coats its sharp edge. My blood. Or his. My stomach cramps at the thought of our blood mixing because of his sick obsession.

I'm not sure if this is a trick question. If I say yes, will he actually untie me and hand me the knife? Hesitation makes me sweat as I mull over my options. If I say no, will he continue cutting until there's nothing left to keep him from touching me? But if I say yes, will he find another cruel way to punish me?

My lungs burn as I take a deep breath. This feels like being eighteen all over again and staring down two opposite paths: stay with the family who took my mother from me, or run as far away as my heels can carry me. But that kind of thinking is too narrow; there are more options in front of me than I realize. If I had understood back then that if option A and option B didn't work for me, I could have created an option C, maybe I could have stayed *and* demanded more for myself.

Maybe, I could have avoided meeting Liam in the first place.

I stare at the knife in his hands and ignore the panic fluttering inside my ribcage. I don't have to play Liam's games. I can choose another outcome.

"You're a fucking coward, you know that?"

Liam's wicked expression freezes before my eyes.

I glare up at his crooked nose. I'm glad Ezra beat the shit out of him, after all. He deserves an ugly face to match his rotten heart. "What is it my grandmother said?" I tilt my head, pretending to think about it. "That you had *five years* to secure me? And you failed, didn't you?"

"I didn't fail." Liam's words come out stilted. "I *have* you, Valentina. You're mine."

I shrug one shoulder as best I can beneath my bindings.

"You may have my body tied to this chair, but there's no other part of me you'll ever own. Not my name, not my heart, *nothing*. You'll die sooner than you think, and no one will remember you, not even me. So I think, by those standards, you *have* failed, Liam."

The silence is broken by Mikhail's laughter. "Oh, *I'll* remember him. His beating heart in my hands will be a sweet memory to keep me warm on cold winter nights."

My gaze shifts from Liam over to my boyfriend's picture on the screen. "That'll be me warming your bed, love, not memories of this fucking coward."

Liam's expression darkens, his frozen smile cracking at the edges. "Don't test me, Valentina. You won't like what happens."

Anger sizzles beneath my skin at the threat. What *more* could the bastard do to me than humiliate me like this? "What, are you gonna take a picture of me and jerk off to it in the corner?"

I don't see the slap coming. I *should*. He's hit me before. But being tied up and pissed off while your boyfriends watch on screen can really make a woman overlook those important details.

My head whips to the side with a loud *crack*, dark spots dancing in my vision. A shout from the speaker fills the room, drowning out the thundering of my heart.

Liam's breathing has gone ragged. He grabs a fistful of my hair and yanks my head back up, leering down at me. "Watch your mouth, *zhena*. I'd hate for your pretty face to match mine tonight." A few seconds pass, and he takes a breath, visibly composing himself. A flicker of remorse crosses his face as he examines the mark he's made on my cheek, gingerly pressing the pads of his fingers to my hot, swollen flesh. "You shouldn't be cruel, Valentina, or I'll lose my temper. I want to be a good husband to you. Try not to make it a difficult job."

I ignore his attention and refocus on the screen. I will Mikhail to hurry up and find me. And *Ezra*. Where is he?

Mikhail must sense my question because he shakes his head and mouths *no*.

I guess I'm not meant to bring attention to the fact that one of my boyfriends has dipped from the video feed. Hopefully, he's tracking my location the longer we're online.

Liam sighs and releases my hair. "Katya will be cross that you're marked. But, we're supposed to be on our honeymoon. No one needs to see you for a week, at least. Not even Katya." He lowers his lips to my swollen cheek and presses a gentle kiss there. "I suggest you behave, or our honeymoon will be a painful memory for you."

Ice trails down my spine, dousing any fire left within me. I can handle a little smack here or there. The knife . . . is concerning, I'll admit, but he shouldn't get carve-happy. I need to keep a pretty face or the Bratva will revolt against our so-called marriage.

Liam's fingers play with the ragged edges of my bodice. "Unless you enjoy a little pain with your pleasure, *zhena*. I'll admit, it's not something we've tried before . . . but I'll do anything to please you." His lips ghost over the shell of my ear, sending goosebumps down my arms. His voice rasps in my ear, low and menacing. "Did you let them fuck you, Valentina? Have you been a naughty girl while I've been gone?"

My heart beats wildly in my chest. *No.* That's where I draw the line. *Right there.* I can handle a little physical violence. I can stomach being called a whore or a bitch or whatever else Liam can come up with.

I *won't* tolerate anything in the realm of *sex*.

"This isn't a real marriage." I pull at the rope binding my wrists, gritting my teeth against the pain. If I could just get a hold of the knife— "This is *not* a honeymoon. We are *not* sharing any sort of—" I bite my tongue, forcing myself to stop.

The words *marriage bed* and *wedding night* cut deep. I had plans for tonight that didn't involve my ex-boyfriend forcing himself on me.

That might be the one thing that truly breaks me.

To my horror, a familiar slickness pools between my thighs, Andrei's voice echoing in my head. *I know fear gets you off.* My stomach cramps, and I clench my eyes shut. This is *not* happening. This is not *fucking* happening.

My lip trembles and hot tears pool in my eyes. I don't want to be a victim. I want to be a badass.

I want to be a *queen.*

Queens don't cry. Not once did I ever see my mother or grandmother cry about anything. It's my first unofficial day on the job, and I'm already failing at it.

"*Malyshka.* Look at me."

If Liam heard a word I said, he ignores it, grabbing my bodice and tearing the rest open to bare my chest to him. Once it's out of the way, he grabs a handful of my skirt and tugs, ripping what he can and cutting the rest.

"Valentina. *Look at me.*"

I force my eyes open, but I can't see Mikhail through my tears. I blink rapidly until they clear and I can see my boyfriend's face. His jaw is tight, the anger in his eyes burning hot. "Count your tears," he reminds me, "and we'll make him suffer for every single one. Won't we, Ezra?"

A grunt through the speaker lets me know Ezra is still there. My heart seizes painfully. I suddenly wish they were anywhere else. I draw a breath, but I don't know what to say. I can't ask them to leave. I don't want them to stay, but I don't want to be alone with Liam, either.

Once my skirt is torn away, all that's left are my lacy white panties—the ones I'd saved especially for tonight. I clench my thighs together, but it's no use. Liam shoves them apart, cool air greeting the apex of my thighs and making me shiver.

I wait for something to happen.

I pray I'm about to pass out.

A snarl fills the air as Liam backs away from me, looking angrier than I've ever seen. He tosses the knife to the floor and runs both hands through his hair. "You're fucking *bleeding*, Valentina. For fuck's sake."

The cuts on my chest sting. Of course I'm bleeding. He fucking cut me.

But then I feel it—a deep cramp in my gut, an unmistakable scent in the air, a wetness down there that can only mean—

"I'm on my period." I gasp in a breath as relief floods my system, fresh tears springing to my eyes. I'm not turned on. *I'm on my period.*

Liam looks *offended*, like I'd planned for this. In all our years together, he never initiated sex while I was on my period, and I never asked. It seems like that's his limit.

I'm eternally grateful for it.

He presses the pads of his thumbs to the back of his eyelids and sighs. "You know, I was really looking forward to tonight. You just *had* to go and ruin it."

I can't control when I'm on my period, but if I could, I'd bleed for the rest of my life if it meant Liam would never touch me.

"But—" His eyes snap open. "This *does* mean I'll be the one putting a baby inside you, after all." He licks his lips and the corners of his mouth lift. "No more condoms for us, Valentina. After all, we're *married* now." He shakes his head with a small laugh. "I indulged you with them in the past, but there's no reason for it now. As soon as you're done bleeding —" his face twists with disgust "—I'm filling that womb of yours with my seed. Then we'll see who your body belongs to once you're bearing *my* child." He crosses to the tablet and sneers at the screen. "Say goodbye, boys. Show's over. I'm going to enjoy filling up *my* wife with *my* cum very soon. But you won't be around to see it." He sighs. "A shame, honestly. I'd love for you to hear her scream my name as I knock her up."

"You won't touch her," Mikhail growls. "I'm going to kill you before you get the chance."

Liam glances at me over his shoulder. "How long's your period last, baby? Five days?"

"Seven." I practically scream the word. "Seven days. Not five. I'm a heavy bleeder." I can't believe we're talking about this. But if it keeps Liam off of me for longer, I'll gladly tell him it lasts a whole damn month. "Sometimes it lasts two weeks."

Best not push my luck too much.

"Seven days," Liam repeats, a smile lighting up his face. "Think you can find us in seven days, boys?" He laughs like he's telling the funniest joke in the world, clearly underestimating who he's up against.

My men haven't clawed their way to the top of the Bratva on an old lady's name and connections. They did it themselves.

Mikhail's eyes brighten, and he licks his lips as the gambler in him comes out. "Let's make a bet, Liam. We find you and Valentina within seven days, and as long as you haven't touched a single hair on her head, we take Valentina and let you go."

Liam crosses his arms. "You won't win. It's impossible for you to find us—"

"If *you* win, we'll let Valentina go, and we won't come after you anymore."

All the air in my lungs *whooshes* out at once.

What is he saying?

I wait for Ezra to counter, but the man stays silent, either too busy with whatever the fuck he's doing in the background, or too shocked—*like me*—to say anything.

Liam takes a moment to mull over the endless possibilities in front of him. *A wager.* The stakes being, oh, not much except *my life* handed to the winner on a silver fucking platter.

Liam's smile seems genuine. "If you don't find us within seven days, you have to watch as I fuck Valentina. You don't get to stop me, and you let me walk away with her once we're done. You won't come after me or her, ever again." Liam's actually *interested.*

What the *fuck.*

Mikhail grins, his eyes sharp as he nods. "You've got a deal. Seven days. Starting tomorrow."

"Today."

"*Tomorrow.* In case you've forgotten, you wrecked a fucking wedding. Wrapping that up took most of our day." Mikhail scowls. "It starts tomorrow, or the deal is off, and we find you *and* gut you alive. Your choice."

I can't believe this is happening. I can't believe *Mikhail* is betting my fucking life in a pissing match. I'm going to *strangle* him when I see him.

Liam grumbles, but nods. "The countdown begins at midnight tonight." He glances over at me, his eyes hooded with desire. A rigid tent in his pants makes me gasp. "Better hurry, or I might change my mind. She's *begging* to get fucked when she's tied up like that."

While Liam's distracted, Mikhail meets my eyes, looking more confident than ever. He winks, and my desire to strangle him turns into a *need*.

I'm going to murder the fucking maniac.

The video feed cuts out, and my image in the camera expands to fill the screen. I stare at the naked woman with pity and fury and grief swirling within my heart.

Pity for her fucked-up situation.

Fury towards the men that put her here.

Grief for innocence lost.

Life within the Bratva put me here. It groomed me for a throne without teaching me the shadows that throne sits upon, hiding the blood and bone from view.

I was never meant to look down and see it.

But as I sit naked in a concrete prison, an obsessed psychopath keeping me captive, all I can see is the ruin around me. I'm *within* the shadows now, the part I was never meant to see, the throne high over my head and out of reach.

If my men clawed their way out of the shadows to claim the throne, it's about time I learned to do the same.

CHAPTER 2

VALENTINA

"VALENTINA, VALENTINA, VALENTINA," Liam hums, shaking his head. "My, what a mess you've made of things." He licks his lips as his eyes travel down my body, then his gaze freezes between my thighs. With a sigh, he picks up the switch-blade he tossed to the floor. "I think you need some time to reflect on your behavior, don't you?"

I blink through my unshed tears until they fall from my lashes, clearing my vision and bringing me face to face with my reflection in the tablet screen. Pain lances through my chest at how utterly *violated* I look, and I draw a shaky breath, tearing my gaze away to return Liam's stare. I don't know what he wants me to say. *Yes*, I've been a bad girl, or *no*, I think you're full of shit.

I know I should pick the safest option, but I'll do anything to keep Liam away for longer. If it takes his anger to make that happen, so be it.

I swallow, but it does nothing to ease my dry throat. "I think *you* need a reality check. You can't keep me locked up down here for an entire week." I jerk my shoulders, tugging at my bindings. The chair legs scrape an inch across the floor.

The damned fool never bolted the thing down, which means that he's either inexperienced at this, or he had to make do with what he had in a pinch.

Tying me up might not have been planned, after all.

"Did you expect me to come with you willingly?" I laugh hard enough that I fight a coughing fit as fresh tears spring to my eyes. "You *actually* think I'd choose you over them?"

The corner of Liam's lips twitch. "You chose me before. You'll choose me again." He crosses the distance between us and bends at the waist until we're eye level, then brushes his knuckles against my unmarked cheek. "In these next seven days, Valentina, you'll forget all about them. You'll remember the love you have for me, even if I have to pluck out each and every one of your ribs—" his free hand brushes up the ladder of my ribcage—"to pull it to the surface." His fingers idly grab at my chest, like he's imagining reaching inside to grasp my heart in the palm of his hand.

As his eyes travel my naked body, he hums in appreciation, brushing his knuckles against the top of my breast.

My stomach twists in knots, but I swallow all of my disgust to look him in the eye. Saying his name is like forcing poison down my throat, but I do anyway, damn near desperate to shift his attention.

"Liam."

His hand hovers over my breast, twitching with restraint as his blue eyes flick up to my face. There's a thin layer of sweat breaking out across his neck, a hint of pink tinting the shell of his ear.

I focus on his eyes, the same eyes I used to gaze into and wonder what the future held for us. Never in my wildest dreams did I imagine anything like this.

Liam was always meant to be boring, kind, and safe. A fling for fun. Never anything long-term. Just a means to an end. An itch to scratch. A man who would love me enough to overlook my muddied past and keep me content.

Someone to help me forget about Andrei.

As I look into Liam's icy blue eyes, he is all of those things, yet none of them at all. He was never enough for me—was never *meant* to be enough—because I'd already decided the man I *really* wanted, the man who was hand-picked for me, *had* to be wrong. If Andrei wasn't enough, then neither could Liam be.

An ache burrows deep in my chest. I was such a fool back then, taking men at surface level, not looking deep enough to see what dark secrets remain hidden beneath the surface.

I won't be made a fool again.

I glare at my ex as revulsion pulses through my veins, thick, heavy, nauseating.

There's one thing Liam needs to get through his thick fucking skull. Well, *two* things, but I don't have a bullet to give him right now.

I hold my breath as he leans in close enough to kiss. My resolve hardens alongside the air trapped in my lungs. When our lips brush, I finally speak my mind. "I will *never* love you. Seven days or seven lifetimes—nothing will change that."

Liam hovers over my lips, a low hum catching in the back of his throat. I thought he'd be angry at me for rejecting him, but it's like I barely dented his armor. It still shines bright against the whites of his eyes. "Resist all you like, *zhena,* but in time, you'll remember how we used to be. How good we are together." He lowers his lips to my jawline, curving against it with featherlight kisses. A shiver rolls down my spine, and I clench my fists to keep from shaking. Disgust roils in my gut as his breath ghosts across my face.

"I can be a generous man, Valentina, and an even better husband . . . if you'll let me."

When he dares to press a kiss to the corner of my lips, I

close the distance and capture his mouth, surprising him with a *real* kiss. I suck his bottom lip between mine, and when I feel some of the tension in his body ease, I bite down hard. Copper spills into my mouth, and Liam grabs the first thing he finds—*my neck*. His grip tightens until he closes off my windpipe and makes it impossible for me to breathe.

But I don't dare let go.

With a snarl, he tears his lip free, blood dripping past his lips and staining his chin. He spits, blood and saliva splattering across my face and chest. "I'm going to enjoy taming you," he hisses, "because when you finally submit to me, it will be *exquisite*." He shoves me away from him with a hard push on my neck, releasing my throat and storming to the door.

"Is that all you've got?" A laugh spills from my chest, cracking dryly in my throat. Liam's blood lolls across my tongue, and I swallow it down, letting it ease some of my discomfort. It's not water, but *fuck*, does it ignite a fire in my blood. When I have his attention again, I give him a lazy, lopsided smile as my pulse races through my veins. "My father would have never chosen you, y'know. For *pakhan*."

I know my words have hit their target when Liam's entire body freezes; even his chest stills as he forgets to breathe. No one wants to hear that they're unfit for the title of king, especially from the late king's daughter.

I dig the barb deeper. "You're only holding the crown because my *grandmother* gave it to you. No one is going to respect you, Liam, no matter how much you pretend otherwise." I think back to how easily my grandmother controlled her guards in the rose garden—how they followed her every move, without her even having to say a word.

That is real power. She doesn't have to hide behind anyone to walk these streets. Liam will have to duck and cover with how my men are coming after him.

He's playing a dangerous game, trying to take over an

established criminal empire. A pawn dressed as a king. A pawn from *another* Bratva, seizing power in ours only because he has its future queen hostage.

At least Andrei had the guts to rise to the top on his own goddamn work ethic. He doesn't need my Baranova name to secure power nearly as bad as Liam does.

I can see it in Liam's eyes. The fear. The way it ripples just beneath the surface, betraying any shred of confidence he pretends to have. He doesn't *really* know what he's doing.

And he knows it.

I lick my lips, getting another taste of metal. "If you want power, Liam, *real* power, I can help you get it. We can take it from the one person standing above us in rank. It'll be easy as . . ." I jerk my head to the side, making a cracking sound with my tongue against my teeth. "With Katya out of the way, the Bratva will be looking for its next leader." I incline my head towards him. "Whoever is standing close enough to the throne will get to claim it first. I wonder—" I take a deep breath— "will it be you, Liam?"

Or will it be me?

I've never wanted the throne. It's no secret that a woman, even someone with Baranova blood like me, can't actually claim any power from it. Bratva tradition won't allow it. But Andrei, Mikhail, and Ezra make me *feel* powerful. If I wanted to take a little power for myself, I know they'd willingly give it to me. I could make my own orders. Break a few rules to create new ones.

It's within the realm of possibility when I marry Andrei.

Siding with Liam, on the other hand, will accomplish nothing.

But if I'm going to secure not only my safety, but the safety of the ones I love, there are two people standing in the way. Liam, and my grandmother.

It's only a matter of time before Liam dies. He's a temporary nuisance, in the grand scheme of things. But Katya can slip away easily, blending into the shadows to disappear like smoke. If she does, there's no telling when she'll try this bull-shit again, putting targets on our backs and setting the boun-ties high.

I never wanted her to die, but I don't think I have a choice anymore. With the list of traitors holding knives against my back growing by the day, I can't risk it—not when she's already cut me deep. Her knife is the sharpest of all.

Liam eyes me warily from across the tiny room. "You want me to kill your grandmother?"

I have to be smart about how I play this, or he won't believe me. "In the chapel, before our ceremony, you said that all you wanted was me." I bite my bottom lip and look up at him from beneath my lashes. "That none of the rest—the money, the city, the Bratva—none of it mattered." I let my face fall, dragging in a quick breath. "I just want to be sure that you mean it. That you really want *me*, not any of this . . . other stuff."

Killing Katya means that Liam can have all of the power the throne provides. It will be the ultimate test—does he want *me*, or does he want the power that comes from marrying the sole-surviving Baranova heir?

Something softens in Liam's gaze, and he looks away from me to card his fingers through his hair. "Of course I want you, Valentina. That's what all of this is for." He exhales slowly, a muscle in his jaw jumping as he clenches his teeth. Blood trickles down his chin, and he idly wipes it across his sleeve. "I want you more than anything, Valentina. I always have."

Okay. This is good. This, I can work with. It might even be better than the rage. He's too hot-and-cold for me to predict properly, but if I tease out the softer parts of him, maybe those are the pieces I can control.

Maybe together, we can steal the knife from my grandmother's hands and shove it down her throat. *Then* I can turn my men loose on Liam.

Two traitors, one blade.

I take a deep breath, swallowing all of the rage boiling in my gut. He wants a submissive wife. It's a role I've spent years learning to play. I can stomach it for a few days if it means I can claw my way out of this pit and back to my men.

I feign a sad smile. "All anyone seems to want from me is my name. I'm not even sure that—" My breath catches, but it's not fake. These next words *hurt*. "—they'd want me if it was just *me*."

Would my men still love Valentina if she was a no-name nobody from nowhere?

"I was there first," Liam says, jumping in to fill the space between my words with what he wants to hear. He quickly closes the distance between us and kneels at my feet. Kissing each of my knees, he looks up at me tenderly. "I've always been here for the right reasons, Valentina. For *you*. Oh, baby, don't cry."

A tear that I hadn't felt coming slips free. I've never said those words aloud—that my men might want me for my name, and not for who I am. I know the Bratva comes with the territory—that Andrei was promised his position as *pakhan* as part of the deal for marrying me. That's the undeniable truth.

He's also told me that he loves me.

But Mikhail and Ezra *haven't*.

I bite my lip as another tear rolls down my cheek. I'm sure a part of them loves me. I've *felt* it, I think, in the moments we're together. The way they're determined to protect me, with a ferocity vibrating in the timbre of their voices. How they vehemently hate the man kneeling before me. How they hate the way my grandmother lies and schemes—manipulating me to her benefit.

They hate when others abuse me.

Isn't that a form of love?

Liam brushes away my tears as he stands, cradling my cheek in his palm. "You can trust me, baby. Be good to me, and I'll be good to you. Don't you remember how good we were? How well I've treated you all these years?" He leans his forehead against mine, puffing a breath against my lips. "They've gotten you all confused, putting lies in your head." His lips curve into a snarl, and when he pulls back to search my eyes, the rage from earlier has returned to the surface.

I'll need to be *really* careful with how I handle him.

I close my eyes, part of me shriveling up inside at how vulnerable it makes me. I hold on to the feeling, stacking it neatly beside the rest of my emotions. The fear. The anger. The pain. When it comes time to shove my blade through Liam's wretched heart, I'll sharpen it first, striking the metal against every single vile feeling he's given me until it *zings*, sharp enough to slice through stone.

My voice is soft when I reply. "I don't know. Maybe."

Sighing, Liam presses a kiss to my lips, smearing more of his blood across them. He runs his finger through the sticky mess, painting my mouth red with the taste of him. "If I undo your ropes, will you behave?" His eyes narrow as he considers this. "If you fight me, you're staying here tonight."

I don't want to be tied to a hard-ass chair all night. My ass is already threatening to go numb.

"I'll be good."

This mollifies him well enough that he carefully undoes every knot tying me in place. It takes longer than it should, because he delicately rubs every single patch of raw skin beneath the ropes, running his palms up my arms, my calves, down my back—everywhere he can touch, as though he's saying *sorry*.

But I know better. He's not sorry at all.

He's playing the same game I am, trying to win the other one over. The difference between us, however, is that deep down, he believes he can convince me to stay with him. That if he shows enough compassion and generosity after inflicting pain and punishment, that I'll learn to follow the rules. That he truly can be a *good husband* to me.

I want none of that bullshit.

I only want freedom, and it's a price I'll pay in blood. His. Katya's. Anyone else's who gets in my way. I'm under no delusion that this threadbare peace between us will turn into anything permanent. I'm not here to stay.

And I have seven days, at most, to break free.

CHAPTER 3

VALENTINA

THE UPGRADE from a concrete prison to the master bedroom is jarring, even more so when Liam casually undoes his tie and steps out of his shoes, like we really *are* a married couple preparing for bed after a long day. I watch him for any signs of weakness—any physical tells that he's favoring a leg or got a bullet hole in his arm—but all I find aside from the healing purple and yellow bruises around his eyes, courtesy of Ezra, is a patch over his shoulder. He doesn't wince when he moves, but he's more delicate about rotating his shoulder or lifting his left arm.

I'd bet on *that* being his stab wound from Mikhail.

But if he holds a grudge against me for it, he doesn't show it. Instead, he studies me just as closely as I'm studying him. "You should shower before getting into bed, Valentina."

My skin is sticky with sweat, and I desperately want to clean the blood from not only my chest, but between my thighs. I clutch Liam's suit jacket tighter, begrudgingly grateful for it even though it came from the enemy. It's all I have to wear now, aside from my bloodied panties.

My wedding dress wasn't salvageable after Liam took a

knife to it. The remnants litter the basement floor, sad strips of fabric and lace, evidence of a dream ruined.

I know Liam has seen me naked a hundred times now, but it doesn't make it any easier to willingly undress in front of him. Especially after how forceful he was downstairs.

There isn't a hint of remorse in his eyes as I slowly, nervously, fidget out of my clothes. He must know I'm uncomfortable about being naked in front of him, but my discomfort isn't what bothers him.

It's my lack of desire to return his affection that does.

I can see it in the clench of his jaw, the way his muscles tighten as I try to shrink in on myself. His gaze sweeps across my body, but he doesn't move closer, inclining his head toward the bathroom. "You first, love."

My heart *pangs* at the endearment. First, Liam stole the word *zhena* from Andrei, and now he's stolen *love* from Mikhail. I'll be listening for the moment he takes the word *lisichka,* the knife in my heart burrowing deeper with it.

Taking a deep breath, I steel my spine and walk tall as I step into the bathroom. I need to pretend this is normal. That being with Liam isn't gut-wrenching, but something I want. That I'm only a little nervous about it, instead of wanting to crawl out of my skin every time he comes near.

He leans against the bathroom counter as I shower, eyes dark and lidded as I scrub my body clean. The glass door is fogged from the steam, but I'm under no illusion that he isn't watching close enough to see a peek of nipple or glimpse of creamy thighs beneath the streams of water.

I'm surprised when he hands me a fluffy white towel once I step out of the shower. I'm even *more* surprised when he shows me where the feminine products are and tucks me into bed when the nighttime routine is done. Teeth brushed, hair rolled up in a towel, matching silk pajamas hanging off our hips, and a gentle goodnight kiss on the lips.

I expect Liam to slip into bed beside me and pull me against his bare chest, but instead he watches me from the couch against the far wall. Not lying down, feigning sleep— but sitting up, elbows perched on his knees, chin resting on clasped hands.

Staring.

It's because of this that don't get a single moment's rest, despite how bone-tired I am. My entire body aches, and despite the water I drank from the bathroom sink, my tongue sticks to the roof of my mouth. Side effects from the drugs, or the stress, or the struggle I put up when Liam dragged me out of the chapel this afternoon.

It's all extremely uncomfortable, but somehow my heart is grateful for the shower, the clothes, the bed, and *especially* the fact that Liam is keeping his distance.

It must be part of his plan to win me over. Be nice to me, and maybe I'll roll onto my back for him. He could easily climb into bed, force me in any position he favors, and claim my mouth in a searing kiss, grinding his cock against my slit until he comes in thick ropes across my stomach. He could do *more* than stare at me from across the room.

But he doesn't.

And that makes me even *more* nervous. I'm waiting for the other shoe to drop. For the snap of his sanity. For something to push him over the edge, make him *angry*.

This soft version of Liam is reminiscent of days past, when we'd shared a bed in his high-rise apartment and overlooked the twinkling city from beneath the sheets, sipping wine and making love intermittently until dawn. But that version of him is a lie. The *real* Liam stalks me across state lines, threatens me with violence when I say something he doesn't like, and gets furious and possessive at the idea of another man touching me.

I'm waiting for that man to make his appearance.

The minutes tick by in agony, the sharp cramps in my gut only amplifying my misery. He left a bottle of painkillers on the nightstand—but I don't dare touch them. He's drugged me once; I won't put it past him to do it again.

I'm still waiting when the sun finally rises. He stands, coming round to my bedside to press a gentle kiss to my temple. I hold my breath as he whispers sweetness in my ear.

Sweet dreams, Princess.

I keep holding my breath as he leaves the room, not moving a muscle until I'm sure he's not coming back.

Then, my planning begins. I throw off the blankets and survey the entire room from top to bottom.

Although the color scheme differs from my room at the Baranova estate, the layout is similar enough that it's familiar, and I go through everything systematically: the matching mahogany nightstands, the paneled dresser, the walk-in closet, the granite bathroom, the six inches of clearance under the bed, the safe tucked in the corner of the room whose passcode I can't guess correctly, and the double-wide balcony over-looking the front lawn.

As I step out onto it, warm sunlight paints my skin, but the harsh chill of autumn tears away any comfort it might bring. I shiver and clutch my arms to my chest, peering out at the front drive that curves toward a gleaming silver gate, which leads out into the city. Cars are already zipping by, and despite the barrier of trees at the edge of the property, I can still hear the bustle of the city on its daily commute to work.

Although my life is far from normal, in a way, this fucked-up situation *is* normal for me. It's my day-to-day, sitting at the precipice of life and death, waiting to see which one of us falls over the edge first. I would laugh if I wasn't so upset about it. I'll never have a normal nine-to-five job, be the soccer mom picking her kids up after practice, or be able to grab my favorite coffee on the way into the office every morning.

For a while during those five years I spent away from my father and the Bratva, I tried to have a normal life. Liam was a part of that attempt, and only now do I see how foolish it was to think my home life wouldn't follow me outside city limits. Everything in my life has been coordinated, from the dresses I wear to the people I meet.

It shouldn't be a surprise that meeting—and dating—Liam was yet another string being pulled, a manipulation tactic at its finest. My grandmother has always been a master of the art, it seems, luring not just me, but Liam into her web. We're both pawns in something bigger, but I don't yet know what the end game is. I'm likely not meant to know, as is tradition for a mafia wife to remain naïve.

But if I can get Liam to talk, even if he doesn't know the full scope of Katya's plans, I can piece them together myself. By the time my men find me, I need to have enough information to be useful. I'm not strong like Ezra, tactical like Andrei, or maniacal like Mikhail. But I *am* a Baranova, and that gives me more power than I've ever tried to use.

Leaving the balcony, I take a quick shower and pick an outfit that exemplifies the princess role—a pale pink sundress with an off-the-shoulder cut and a perfect bow at the back. It's not in season at all, but I slip on a pair of white flats and braid my hair over my shoulder to keep up appearances. The house should be warm enough to make this work, and if not, everyone will simply have to deal with seeing my nipples hardened to chilly points all afternoon.

Everything I try on fits perfectly. I bet I'm supposed to be grateful for the foresight and planning that went into my wardrobe.

But all it is, really, is another act of control. I'm not able to pick my own outfits—my husband has already chosen the set. I merely get to pick my costume for the day.

It burns me up even more.

The cuts down my chest from last night are still healing, but the dress hides them from sight. I carefully wedge a wad of toilet paper inside my bra to protect the deepest ones from sweat throughout the day, grit my teeth at the sting, and meticulously apply a natural makeup palette and a steady swipe of eyeliner that accentuates my eyes. The deep green of my eyes pops against the pink of the dress, making me look like a spring blossom waiting to be plucked. A brush of gloss across my lips finishes the look.

I take a deep breath and try the door to the hall. To my surprise, it opens without any resistance, and I push through with a startled *oh.* The first thing I see makes my spine straighten instantly—a guard in full black, his face hidden behind a mask, stands directly opposite me.

"Good morning." I try for a smile that I hope hides my surprise.

The man inclines his head but doesn't verbally reply. I try not to stare at the rifle cradled in his arms. This guard isn't as large as Ezra—likely doesn't have the muscle mass—but he looks no less formidable when he's covered head to toe in padded armor and shielded plating. It's like he's expecting an army to bulldoze through here or something.

I smile a little wider. "Are you my escort for the day?" I know the guards back at the estate are instructed not to speak, but maybe this one will be different. Maybe, for once, I can have a guard on *my* side. I don't have money to bribe him with, but a pretty smile from the lady of the house can go a long way.

To my delight, he nods.

"Excellent." I clap my hands together. "My name is Valentina. What should I call you?"

He doesn't respond, which isn't surprising, so I hum to myself as I think of what to call my masked stranger. "I think I'll call you Riot. Is that alright?" I was trying to think of something more charming that might win him over, but I'll never remember it. Instead, I simply pick what I won't be able to forget: man in riot gear equals the name *Riot*. It's not very creative, but it'll stick.

Now I just have to remember how to pick him out from a crowd of men in matching gear. But maybe that'll come to me later.

"Do you know where my—" I try not to visibly gag on the next word—"husband is?"

Riot stares blankly at me. Great.

I keep a smile on my face. "I was hoping to bring him some breakfast. He left pretty early this morning. Is he in the house? Maybe in his office?"

Still, Riot doesn't respond, so I give up that endeavor. "Alright, well maybe you can point me in the direction of the kitchen so I can grab something for myself?"

A slight head tilt to his right.

I head in that direction, and he follows like a faithful guard dog. I try not to let his presence get to me. Looking over my shoulder at him, I toss him a wink. "Maybe we can get you something sweet for helping me."

God, flirting with the enemy is weird. Dread sinks in the pit of my stomach as I think about flirting with Liam next. I can't go full-in with it or he might suspect something's up, but I won't be able to reject all of his advances, or he might lash out. I resist the urge to chew my bottom lip as we head down a flight of stairs, then another hallway, until finally, a grand staircase leads to the main floor. I track each turn we take, trying to memorize the layout of the house.

As I sweep down the main stairs, brushing my palm along the mahogany railing in a careful glide, two of the guards on patrol stop to watch my descent. I smile sweetly at them, and they continue moving.

There are *way* too many armed guards in here for my

liking. I understand Liam being cautious since my men are likely hunting him as we speak, but this feels overkill. How many guards are his, and how many are my grandmother's?

Speaking of my grandmother, where the hell is she?

I take the opposite direction of the two patrolling guards and check each room, confirming the number of guards and windows I saw on my way upstairs last night. Too many of one and not enough of the other. When I come across a set of closed double doors, muffled voices catch my attention, a mix of English and Russian coming through. Another guard flanks the entrance.

This isn't the kitchen, but it's *something*.

Turning to Riot, I gesture towards the door. "Is this my husband's office?" When he doesn't respond, I turn on my smile. "Do you think you could have a coffee tray and some, oh, croissants or something delivered? Bagels, maybe? They must be hard at work in there."

Per Princess rules, it's not my place to interrupt a meeting when I'm not invited. But a queen can follow a different set of rules, especially one who brings treats.

To my delight, Riot unclasps a radio from his waist and mutters an accented *coffee and bagels to the office* into the receiver. Someone replies with confirmation, and I clasp my hands in front of me as we wait. "Thank you."

He inclines his head. Maybe we're getting somewhere.

I hear the treat cart before it arrives, wheeling down the hardwood, the silver clattering on top. The staff member notices me and pales, and it takes me a moment to understand why.

She was working at the Baranova estate. "Tessa," I greet, swallowing my surprise. *What the hell are you doing here?* "How lovely to see you. I didn't know you worked for my husband."

She gives me a tense smile. "I work for the Madame,

Princess. She requested that I relocate upon your recent nuptials."

My fingers twitch, so I clutch them tighter together. "The Madame sent you here." *Of course* Katya snaked her way into the estate. I wonder if she gave word the day she paid me an unexpected visit. *Follow me or die*, or something just as extreme.

Everything around here feels like it's life or death.

I take a step closer to Tessa. I don't dislike the girl; hell, I hardly even know her. *But still.* A precedent needs to be set, and she's the first person I've come across to set one. To her credit, she holds her ground. She's older than me, likely having worked for the Baranovas a long time. I can't fault her for following Katya's orders.

But it means she went against her *pakhan*. And I need to win her loyalty back for us.

"As you've heard of my wedding, I'm sure you're aware that I am no longer simply a princess." I keep my smile sweet, but by the way she flinches, I can tell she sees that she's struck a nerve. "I thank you for following the *previous* Madame, but I believe that title now belongs to me. As the current Madame, I hope to see you following orders just as swiftly for me as you did for her." I set my hands on the cart. "Thank you for bringing the tray I ordered. It's perfect."

As I tug on the cart, Tessa holds on just as tight, not letting me move. "I can take this inside for you—"

"*Tessa.*"

She flinches at the warning in my voice.

"What were you asked to do?"

She blinks at me, her lips pressing into a thin line. "Bring coffee and bagels to the office."

"That's right." I nod. "Nothing was said about taking the tray inside. I'd hate for you to misstep and tarnish that perfect record of yours so soon. We're just getting started, after all, when we have years of service ahead of us."

She finally lets go of the cart. "Yes, Madame."

"Wonderful. You're dismissed." I look to Riot next. "Would you be a dear and open the door for me? I'd like to bring my husband a little surprise treat."

Riot hesitates, likely choosing sides. If he's been ordered to follow me around, he may have been ordered to keep me away from business discussions and the like. But I'm curious whose orders he's following—Liam's as the *alleged* new *pakhan*, or Katya's as the Madame.

When he steps in front of me to pull open the double doors, I get my answer.

He's following *mine.*

CHAPTER 4

VALENTINA

THE FIRST THING I notice is that the room is filled with men. *Older* men, like, as old as my dad would be, were he alive. Some are better matched to my grandmother, with gray hair and deep-set wrinkles carved around their eyes and mouths, one of them even sporting a cane set down by his side. Everything about them screams old money and privilege—from the way they glare at me as I enter the office, to the obnoxious shine on their leather shoes.

The decor matches its guests; dusty bookshelves with ancient tomes line two walls, with a heavy, wooden desk sitting at the far side. Liam sits behind it as leader of this gathering, with the other men lounging on couches or in armchairs around the room.

A dozen men, and one frigid old bitch lurking in the corner.

I enter the room as quietly as possible, but the clatter of the silver serving fork on the equally shining silver tray, combined with the rattle of coffee mugs against a sleek metal carafe, means I fail miserably. Not that it would have mattered with Riot following me inside; the broad set of his shoulders could block out the sun, and he takes up double the space of the older men. If they don't notice me, they definitely notice the tall, imposing guard disobeying his *pakhan's* orders by allowing me inside.

The chatter in the room ceases instantly as all eyes fall upon Riot and me, and I can't help but imagine this as some all-boys' party I've crashed—like I snuffed out the birthday boy's huge *look at me* candle, and now everyone's waiting to watch him explode at the woman who ruined his big moment.

Liam may have mastered his poker face, but there's no mistaking the steely glint in his cerulean eyes. He's *pissed*.

I smile sweetly at him as I wheel the cart to the center of the room. "I hope you boys will excuse the interruption. My husband left so early this morning—why, I thought he might need a little pick-me-up after such a long night."

A few of the men smirk, and the sudden rush of heat across my cheeks is one hundred percent authentic. I worked hard to cover the bruise Liam left on my cheek, but it aches the longer I stand here smiling. Carefully, I pour Liam his perfect cup of coffee: black with two sugars, mindful not to make a mess.

Our eyes meet when I look up, and I can *feel* it—the challenge I've presented him, draped across my shoulders like a heavy cloak. Will he entertain this interruption to business, or will he punish me for it?

And, if he punishes me in front of all these men, will I fight back? Can I withstand the humiliation of a public spanking—or *worse*?

While Liam makes his decision, I carefully lean across the desk to set his coffee in front of him, giving him an ample glimpse of cleavage in the process.

To his credit, he doesn't even look at my boobs, too focused on holding my gaze.

Were this a normal day and a normal relationship instead

of some fucked-up hostage kink-fest, I might be insulted. I've got great tits.

"Darling," I greet, sweetening my smile. "Would you like anything else?"

His nostrils flare, but after a tense heartbeat, he averts his gaze, dismissing me to return to conversation with the man beside him. Still, he clutches his coffee mug, thumbing its side idly, as I take a tour of the room and greet each of its inhabitants with a smile and a sweet treat.

Most of the men pay me little mind, their mouths pinched, their responses curt. When they don't accept coffee or a bagel, the rejection stings exactly how it's meant to—as an *offense.* These men are actively offending me by refusing my generous gift. They want me to know how little they think of me. They want me to learn my place beneath their heels.

I know where they want me. I've been trained my whole life on how to be the perfect lap dog—pretty, but insignificant.

But I have better plans for my life.

I take turns giving each man in the room attention, placing my hand on one's forearm as I ask his coffee preference, bending slightly to address another, murmuring softly as I get the attention of a few at the edges of the room. Of the twelve men, some I actually recognize as my father's business associates. About half of them are new, with only two of them looking young enough to be in their thirties.

They're the ones who watch me move around the room instead of listening to the business at hand, which makes it difficult for me to eavesdrop. The good thing about Liam's present company is that in order for discussion to reach all ears in every corner of the room, Liam needs to speak up—especially as I tinker with stirring cream and sugar into mugs that no one seems to want. It means that I can multi-task, taking mental notes about the conversation as much as I am about who's in the room.

In addition to all the men, my grandmother's sitting in the corner, completely unobtrusive as she perches in an armchair by an empty fireplace. She blends in so well with the furniture that at first, I nearly overlook the fact that she's here—which, I'm sure, is precisely her goal. When I pass in front of her, the look she gives me could freeze hell over. The firm press of her lips matches the stiffness in her posture. I won't let her win the silent judgement round, so I slather her favorite bagel in cream cheese and bring her a bread plate.

"For you, *babushka*." As I hold the plate over her lap, she takes my hand and squeezes tight. My smile pinches as I avoid reacting.

Her eyes search mine, her lips twitching into a frown. "*Ditya*. I did not expect to see you this morning." Her gaze sweeps over my outfit, her frown deepening.

"Well, a wife is meant to support her husband." I lick the fruity gloss off my lips, smacking them. "What better way than providing for his guests?"

In truth, I wasn't sure who all would be inside the room. Now that I'm here, I'm not sure I should have entered dressed like *this*.

To some people, a woman is merely a target, something to tease and touch as they please. A pretty woman in a dress, oozing sweetness like me, is damn near irresistible. That was the point of this little ensemble—to catch eyes and attention, to let them know that I'm not going to sit in the corner and wait to be called upon—and it's clear that, for the two youngest associates, at least, it's working.

They're *hungry*, and they've just spotted their next meal. As I approach the first of the two men, I can't help but feel like Little Red Riding Hood approaching the Big Bad Wolf, my basket of treats in hand, while the monster drools at the temptation in front of him.

Me.

As I'm readying a new plate for the next guest, Liam chooses that moment to speak up, the word *orphanage* stealing my attention away from my hands. I distractedly push a bagel off the tray and onto the floor, the soft *thud* lost to me over the words booming through the room.

"If we don't have enough men, we'll simply take more. How many are housed there?"

"They aren't ripe enough yet. Some are barely fifteen, *pakhan.* They can't even handle their own dicks, let alone a gun."

"A fifteen-year-old can be taught to shoot."

"We don't have that kind of time—"

Fingertips brush the inside of my wrist, jerking my attention back into my body. My heart races as the man beside me sets the fallen bagel back onto the cart, his other hand hovering over my wrist. "Are you alright, love? You look a little flushed." The pads of his fingers press into my skin, his eyes lighting up as he finds my skittering pulse. "Mm, heart racing, too. Nervous about walking into the lion's den?" He chuckles softly, more to himself than to me, and I blink to focus. *Focus.*

Francesca's name rings in my ears, as do the words *gun* and *training.* What the hell do orphaned kids have to do with either of those things?

I let my smile slip a moment ago, and I carefully reapply it, giving a smaller, more timid one this time. "I'm a little clumsy today. What can I get you, Mister . . ."

Liam's voice booms like thunder, crashing heavily from above. "If you want to keep that hand, Anton, I suggest you move it before I misunderstand what you're reaching for."

Anton's lips curve into a confident smirk as he releases my wrist, reaching past me for an empty mug. "No offense intended, *pakhan*. Your wife is sweet to dote on us." He licks a stripe across his front teeth, flashing his canines, before glancing at his *pakhan*. "I'm a little jealous, actually. Wish I had a pretty wife waiting on me like this. You're lucky that you're the oldest, brother." His eyes sweep back over to me, darkening as he notices me staring back. "Or you'd be mine, pretty girl."

Liam mentioned siblings once a long time ago, but I never put two and two together, especially not after how crazy everything's been. If Liam's in the mafia, of course his siblings are, too.

As Anton addresses Liam, I can see the familial resemblance in the bright blonde faded cut, the shape of his stubbled jaw, and the fucking insanity for being so casual in a room full of criminals. Criminals who are *glowering* at us.

Anton remains unfazed. He smirks as he takes his seat, likely thinking my blush is for him, but it's not.

I'm fucking *furious*. Embarrassed. Never in my life have I felt so *objectified*, and I see so clearly that this is the life I would have had, if I'd played my role as princess perfectly five years ago. Nothing more than a trophy with a big, wet hole to fill.

Anton taps the empty mug in his hands, waiting for me to pour him coffee. "I like mine full of cream."

One of the old men standing closest to Liam—Kravinsky, I think is his name—laughs. He gestures between the brothers, his voice bitter. "*This* is the family meant to lead us? Fawning over a *woman*?" He tsks, his eyes roaming toward my grandmother. "Allowing the matron in the meeting room, as well. Tolkotsky must be rolling in his grave, God rest his fucking soul."

Liam's jaw tics. "Please, Kravinsky, keep insulting me. I'd be happy to fill your seat at my table. What is it you keep telling me? That your sons are itching for a promotion?" He flicks open a switchblade and stirs his coffee with it, clinking the metal against ceramic. "I can expedite that process *very* quickly."

Kravinsky rears his head back. "Are you mad? We've wiped meaner shits off our asses than you, boy. You may have the title of *pakhan*, but make no mistake—" He juts his finger towards the corner of the room, where my grandmother sits like a statue—"*she* is the one who put you there. It's out of respect for the Madame that we're even here." He bows his head towards Katya, showing deference despite the fact he clearly doesn't think she should be in the room to begin with. "She orchestrated the coup to overthrow that upstart Leonov. Now all *you* have to do is not ruin everything we've built—"

The blade slices through the air so fast that I miss it, only catching the wet gurgle in the man's throat, then the sudden burst of crimson as Liam withdraws the blade from the other man's flesh. Kravinsky clutches his neck, eyes wide, as he chokes on his own blood. He falls to the ground, thumping against the desk on his way down.

Liam wipes the blade on his shirtsleeve. "Come here, *zhena*."

I jump at my name, not expecting to hear it. My ears ring as I tear my gaze away from Kravinsky's body and force my legs to move.

I just watched a man die.

It's my first time experiencing death—yet another first that Liam has taken from me—but I know it won't be my last.

I intend for Liam to have that honor *very* soon.

He leans back in his seat, scooting out far enough to pat his thigh and beckon me onto it. Carefully, I do as I'm instructed, perching on his knee. He wraps an arm around my waist and pulls me back against his chest, pecking a warm kiss against my cheek. "Good girl."

My stomach twists as the praise gnaws at me. I've imagined myself sitting in Andrei's lap as he leads our kingdom—

or better yet, as *we* make decisions together—but sitting in Liam's makes me feel less like an equal and more like the dog he expects me to be.

The words *good girl* only heighten that feeling. I half expect him to reach into the desk drawer and pull out a treat.

"Let's make something clear, gentlemen." Liam takes his time meeting the eyes of every man in the room. "You may have your opinions about this Bratva, or its leader, or his wife." His palm digs into my hip, clutching me tighter. "But I don't give a fuck about your opinions. You are here as advisors to ensure we win this fucking war. If you have a problem with how I run things, or whose company I keep, you can follow Kravinsky out the door." With a nod, he silently orders Riot to *clean up the mess.*

A streak of blood follows Kravinsky's body as Riot drags it from the room.

Liam taps his knife on the desk, and from this angle, I can see the map of the city laid out in front of me. Landmarks are highlighted, the Baranova estate colored red, multicolored lines and notations and symbols littered across the page.

I don't have a fucking clue what I'm looking at, but I settle back into Liam and try to appear relaxed as he massages my hip and gets back to business, calling up the next man to advise him on not just our manpower, but our firepower and real estate.

I take it all in—the numbers, the trade routes, the strategy —and make a promise not to forget a single detail.

Even if I have to sit with the devil to do it.

Chapter 5

Mikhail

I know every single building in this city. Who owns it. Who designed it. Who paid for it. It goes further; I know who owns the land *and* what lies beneath it—whether that be a sewage system or a nuclear bunker or a whole lot of dirt. I know *everything* that happens in this city's real estate, because I own the largest portion of it.

Up until recently, I owned damn near all of it—well, the Monrovia family does, and as its head of house, that means *me*.

So when I stare at a building I intimately know, from the architect's name to the construction crew that built the damn thing to its current owner *and* manager, and can't step inside, I'm *pissed*.

"What do you mean I'm barred from entry?" I bare my teeth at the security guard, some guy who *should* be on our payroll but apparently isn't, and try not to laugh. This whole thing is absurd.

"There's a gas leak," the guard tells me, sounding bored out of his mind. I would be too if I got paid to babysit an abandoned warehouse. "Gotta wait for the city inspectors, then the repair crew."

I look past the man to the empty office inside, spotting the still-steaming paper cup next to the half-full coffee pot. There are papers strewn across the admin desk, like whoever was there couldn't clean up before the end of their shift, or before they were kicked out by an alleged hazard.

Or, if they were interrupted by my unexpected arrival.

I flex my hand, stretching my fingers. If Ezra were here, I'd have him tussle with the man to get him out of my way. But seeing as he's not here, and my talents lie elsewhere, I'll have to make do with another tactic.

I reach into my wallet and pull out a wad of cash. I only deal in hundreds, and by the guard's widening eyes, I'd say he knows of my reputation. I can be a generous bastard when I want to be. "You got any kids—" I glance at the name embroidered on his uniform—"Mr. Simmons?"

He clenches his jaw. "You need to leave, sir. This is private property, and like I've told you, no one is allowed inside."

I tap the crisp edge of bills against Billy Simmons' chest, committing his name and face to memory. "On account of the gas leak."

"Yes."

He doesn't move to take the money, so I remove one bill from the stack and tuck it into his shirt pocket. "Alright, then. Give Marcus my regards, will you?" I fold the money back into my wallet and turn to leave, already in the process of calling Andrei when Billy Simmons says something that sets my teeth on edge.

"You didn't hear? Marcus died last week."

The world comes to a screeching halt. Andrei chooses to pick up at that precise moment. "What is it?"

"Marcus is dead," I repeat, lifting my eyes to Billy. "When?"

"Last Tuesday. His brother didn't want the property, so he sold it to some out-of-state guys. The firm handling the estate jumped on it. Marcus' body wasn't even cold yet, man."

"Get the name of the real estate company," Andrei orders, "and every single person on staff, past and present, for them and the warehouse—"

It's clear he's not talking to me, so I pull out a few more bills and tuck them into Billy's shirt pocket. "Who's the new owner?" I'm surprised I didn't hear about any of this, but with how shitty my own real estate company's been performing lately, it's no wonder they missed a competitor swooping in.

"That's above my pay grade."

"Of course it is." My smile tightens. Oh, how I *so* don't have time for this. Andrei's going to have to do some digging, and all the while, our woman is God knows where. Playing these games while Valentina is with Liam is like peeling your own skin off one slow inch at a time. Fucking *unbearable*.

In fact—I *don't* have to do this shit. It takes all of two seconds to slide my phone in my pocket and grab my gun. Billy doesn't have the experience to know that a man like me is always armed—that, or he's just really bad at his job.

Pressing the barrel underneath Billy's chin is like a breath of fresh air. Shouldering him against the glass front door kicks my pulse up a notch, and all of a sudden, things are a lot more tolerable. "If you want to keep your brains inside your skull, Mr. Simmons, I suggest you start talking. What are you really guarding, because let's be honest, it's not this trash warehouse."

Billy's eyes narrow, his entire body tensing as I dig my elbow into his ribs. "Put the gun down, Mr. Monrovia. No one has to die today."

What a stupid, cliche thing to say.

The glass suddenly shatters behind him, so loud that I almost miss the *pop* of a gun beneath the sound of cracking glass. A grunt passes Billy's lips as his body jostles from the invisible bullet, then we both tumble through the doorway and onto the floor. As I push myself up off of his chest, blood bubbles past his lips and his eyes start to fade. Glass cracks under my feet as I duck behind the front counter for cover. Billy stares motionless up at the ceiling, already dead. "Fucking Christ, Andrei, get me some fucking backup!"

His voice sounds from my pocket. "I told you to take a team."

"You know I don't like teams!"

Footsteps thud down the hall, then a door slams open in the distance. Billy's killer is running away.

I jump up to follow. "I'm in pursuit."

"Don't get yourself killed."

"Not planning on it."

The chase begins as I barrel through a door onto the gritty warehouse floor, and one glance at our surroundings confirms that, much like me, my target is working alone. The warehouse is fucking *empty*. Gutted to the studs to undergo some kind of overhaul, which has *not* been approved for a permit. That much, at least, I know.

The killer is still running toward the far end of dock doors, each one shuttered closed. They should have picked a better escape route, but judging by the way they run in a straight line, I doubt they're used to running for their life.

Young, inexperienced, or downright stupid.

Sunlight filters in from the windows way up high near the ceiling, giving the room enough of a glow that I can see through the dust kicking up. Everything is in muted shades of brown and ugly as fuck.

It's a terrible place to die.

As the assailant tries the back door and finds it locked, I slow to a jog to witness their panic. The way they breathe hard through their mouth, jerking their arms around as they try to open not just the regular door but also the closest dock door by hand, failing to notice the pin that keeps it in place. It rattles but doesn't open.

I hold my gun at the ready as I pick my way across dusty debris, careful with where I step. "If you surrender now, I'll make it quick."

Not that they deserve it after killing their own hired help.

I push thoughts of Billy from my mind. I hope he didn't have any kids, after all.

My gun's already raised when they remember theirs, twitching for it. It's a tiny silver thing, shoved into their front pocket. Good aim is what took Billy down, not firepower.

"He didn't have to die, you know. I wasn't going to kill him." I step closer, taking in the baggy cargo pants, the ratty black shirt, the unkempt hair, and *Jesus*, the terror in his dark eyes. I'm not facing a Bratva man with a kill record—he's just a *kid*. Lanky and underfed, from the looks of it.

Billy may have been his first.

His breaths are shallow and fast, like a cornered rabbit, as we stare each other down.

I take a deep breath. "Easy. I don't want to hurt you. I just need to know what you're doing here and who you're working for."

This building *used* to be under our jurisdiction two weeks ago, but when my people somehow *misplaced* our contracts for multiple properties across the city, shit went sideways, and we still haven't recovered. I fired those responsible, but now I'm thinking I was too hasty. Maybe they were paid to sabotage.

Maybe the Madame had gotten to them, too. I think back to all those people at the wedding chapel a few days ago—all those traitors breathing our air and drinking our champagne, laughing and making fools of Ezra, Andrei, and me. Thinking they're going to win. Thinking they're going to take her from us, take our *Bratva*, take our city.

No one can take this city from the people who live and breathe it every day. I was born in Harlin Heights, as was Andrei, and we'll fight for it tooth and nail.

An outsider won't win, especially not someone using children to fight their battles. It reeks of desperation and poor planning, which means that whoever is orchestrating this—Katya, I suspect—doesn't have the resources we think they do.

I stop my advance, frowning at the kid. If he pulls any shit, I'll shoot him in the leg, but I won't kill him. He was probably trying to survive on the streets when he got tangled in Bratva business. Someone must have snatched him up.

"What's your name?"

The door we originally came through opens, and someone flicks on the lights. They sputter to life one click at a time, and the monotones of the room brighten enough for me to see how truly vast the room is without any shelves or scaffolding in the way. You could fit so much shit in here. It's a great place to house munitions, or vehicles, or—

I squint at the boy now that he's bathed in fluorescents. If I thought the room was dirty, I underestimated the kid—he looks like he's been rolling around in dust for days. Dirt's caked on his neck, dusting his clothes and hair, packed under his fingernails—

Ezra appears beside me a moment later, his scowl deep and a muscle in his neck twitching as he eyes the boy. "There are six more in other room. You did not sweep building."

"I was a little preoccupied."

He ignores me, instead speaking Russian to the boy. *How many of you are there?*

The boy's shoulders relax a little, and I realize he's not just a random teenage squatter—he's Bratva born and bred, although not where he should be, if that's the case. If he doesn't have a family, there are plenty of beds at the children's home and a dozen more foster families who would gladly take him in.

So what the *fuck* is a child doing here?

I grit my teeth as I fail to come up with any reasonable scenarios. "What's he doing here, Ezra?"

Ezra ignores me, walking up to the kid and asking him more questions. The boy scratches at his neck, and I realize it's not dirt caked on his skin, but thick-lined tattoos, one of which mirrors Ezra's own ink.

The boy's come straight from Russia. He's not one of ours, or we'd treat him fucking better than this. Anger strikes hot in my chest as the boy hands Ezra his gun and allows the older man to clap him on the shoulder.

I'm privileged in that I was born to a modestly wealthy family in American society. I'm still Bratva—but not like Ezra or Andrei, who were raised in its underbelly. I haven't had to climb my way to the top of any ladders. I've been at the top since my life began—given an advantage because of my family name and position within our organization.

The way the kid glares at me shows that he, at least, understands that much. But if I get to mold this city and its Bratva the way I want—if Andrei gains enough power and influence to truly make changes—we'll work together to ensure none of our people suffer injustices like this.

Living in a fucking *warehouse*.

I scoff aloud and leave Ezra to address the kid on his own. Pulling my phone from my pocket, I'm surprised to see that Andrei's still on the line. "There are kids here. Russian Bratva. Katya likely had them brought over." I enter the front office just in time to watch a clean-up crew zip up Billy in a body bag.

This whole thing is all kinds of fucked up. The kids housed in here didn't even have a proper guard—just some random schmuck out to make some money.

My voice pitches as I hold the phone to my ear. "I want this kid to be the last, Andrei, you hear me? The last one we find like this."

"It's not that simple."

"Make it that simple!" I slam my fist against the wall. "I want Valentina back, but she'll hate us if we have to mow down dozens of kids to get to her." I bet that's Katya's plan— to show Valentina who the true monsters are. Not the woman using kids as a shield, but the men willing to raise weapons against them if it means keeping our wife safe. "Katya's a fucking coward."

"She's desperate. Desperate people make mistakes, Mikhail."

I know what he's implying—we can't be desperate, or we'll risk making a mistake we can't afford. I step outside, avoiding Ezra's team as I head straight for my car. Seeing it reminds me of Valentina in the passenger seat on the day I took her to meet my sister, and my chest clenches tightly.

Once I'm in the driver's seat, I grip the wheel hard enough that my knuckles whiten, trying—and failing—to ignore the throbbing ache beneath my ribs.

"I thought she might be here." I smile bitterly at how foolish the idea was—that she'd be locked away in some warehouse, guarded by one man, and one man alone. "I thought that maybe, maybe this was the one. That she'd be waiting for me inside."

It's the twentieth building I've checked since our video call dropped. The twentieth that's gone off our radar over the past few weeks. There are dozens more. Not all are warehouses, some are apartment buildings, some are random lots and residential homes. I'm not sure when our control started to slip, but what was a mere blip on the radar before has become a nightmare.

Katya has been planning this for a long time. How to misdirect our attention and keep our forces thinned. How to stay hidden. How to steal our fucking Bratva out from under our noses.

Our control has always been . . . tenuous. We grabbed the reins from Tolkotsky's stiff, dead fingers and ran with them, only to realize a few months down the line that not everyone in Tolkotsky's advisory council had our best interests at heart. Some were undermining our orders and giving their own. Some were running drugs we didn't sanction. Some were waiting on a tattooed god to smite the whole city and rebuild everything from scratch.

We eliminated them one by one and regained the ground we had lost, but it took time. Money. Lives. Things we couldn't afford to lose.

Everything would have been so much simpler if Valentina hadn't left. As one of the older Bratva families, the Baranovas have always had an obsession with blood, and following the bloodline for succession has been tradition for as long as the Baranovas have existed. If Valentina had stayed and married Andrei, our ascension wouldn't have been called into question nearly as much as it had.

The fact that we're *still* fighting to keep our empire despite everything we've put into it proves that we've let too much slip from our fingers.

It's put our queen at risk. I wouldn't be surprised if she tries to leave us for good, after this. Not that she *can*. Not that we'll *let* her.

No, Valentina won't be getting away again, and we'll get a chokehold on our fucking Bratva as soon as this bullshit with

Katya is over. When the old woman lies dead at their feet, the dissenting half of the Bratva will realize they put their faith in a brittle promise of the past.

Nothing will be the same, and I'm damn sure looking forward to it.

"It's only a matter of time until we find her." For a man who spent five years searching for his lost bride, Andrei has been very calm about losing her again. Part of that comes with the title of *pakhan*. He can't show weakness, or that he's just as rattled as Ezra and me.

But I'm held to no such standard. I can be as dour about our situation as I want. "It's been two days."

Andrei's silence is suffocating. He hasn't said it, but I know he's angry about my little wager. Seven days may not seem like a lot of time to him, but to me, it's a lifetime. It's a death sentence.

If I can't find Valentina in seven days, I'll go crazy and burn the entire city down, looking for her. Ezra's ping on the video call helped narrow our search to the south side, but it's still like finding a needle in a haystack.

Very fucking annoying.

"Maybe she'll find us," Andrei muses, sounding damn near wistful about it. "Maybe she's already on her way."

"I don't know how you're not losing your fucking mind." I feel like I'm losing mine, and I haven't been in love with her for half a decade.

"I'm confident we'll find her, just like I'm confident Liam will suffer when we do." Andrei may not physically be in the car with me, but his commanding presence lingers. His confidence is contagious, and my heartbeat slows from a fucking jackhammer to something resembling normalcy.

Ezra raps on my passenger window, and I unlock the door for him. He slides in easily, grunting in greeting. "Seven boys total. All speak Russian. They do not yet know loyalty." He scoffs. "First mistake was not training them."

We sit in silence for a moment. None of us have been sleeping, and if we happen to slip unconscious, it doesn't last but a few minutes, at most. We're running off of caffeine and adrenaline, although I have a sneaking suspicion that Ezra is hitting something harder. Something from his soldier days that keeps him wired way too long and way too tight.

He lights a cigarette, and I'm too tired and stressed to yell at him for smoking in my ride.

"Where would snake hide?" Ezra blows out a puff of smoke. "Where would Katya feel safe inside city? She would not leave Valentina alone, or somewhere unsafe."

That's likely true.

"She has friends in high places." I rub my forehead, willing the ache in my skull to subside. "She wouldn't be in bed with just anyone, and she couldn't have made a large purchase without us knowing about it. Anywhere worth living around here is at least one mil."

The former Madame, her chosen usurper, and the true blood heir to the Baranova Bratva won't be hiding in your everyday hotel or house. Our people would be just as likely to find them as we are, if Katya dared put them somewhere within the general public's sphere.

"She's with someone who can hide them in plain sight. Someone with money."

"Or influence," Andrei agrees.

"Or both." Ezra pinches his cigarette between his fingers. "When did you last hear from mayor?"

Andrei's exhale crackles across the speaker. "I haven't heard from him since we left his birthday party last week."

The mayor is an older man, someone from the old guard inducted during Tolkotsky's reign. He has power, and influence, and money. We've been lining his pockets generously, but that doesn't mean he wouldn't turn on us if given the opportunity.

I'm already turning the ignition when Andrei's order comes across the line.

Meet me at his penthouse.

Time to pay the old fucker an unwelcome visit.

CHAPTER 6

VALENTINA

IF I THOUGHT STEPPING into Liam's meetings would teach me something, I was *right*.

So fucking right.

Not only do I have access to all of Liam's plans for overtaking not just the Bratva, but the *city*. Most of the notes written in the margins are in English, but a delicate hand has marked a few pages with Russian words and phrases.

I'd recognize the handwriting anywhere as my grandmother's. Even though she pretends to be the silent observer hiding in the corner of every room in the house, I know she's still pulling invisible strings. I can practically see them floating through the air every time Liam moves.

She's trained him well on what to say. I'll give her that much.

Outside of the meetings, however, Liam takes the time to show me our new home a little more each day. It gives me unprecedented access to his schedule, so I know exactly what he's up to and where he is at all hours of the day. It's rare that we're not together, and the staff and house guests start to expect my presence as much as their *pakhan*'s.

It makes planning for an escape that much more difficult.

There are a few moments I have to myself, though, whenever Liam leaves the grounds. He takes a handful of guards with him and disappears for hours. I don't know what he's doing or where he's going—all I know is that I suddenly find myself with *time*.

I use every second of it to carefully roam the house for its best-kept secrets. The easiest ones to find aren't those written on paper, much to my surprise.

It's the ones embedded into the estate itself—from its well-kept staff to the very foundation it's built upon—that spills the most information.

I was right when I noticed it before; the entire grounds are a replica of the ones I grew up in, from the shade of paint on its walls to the type of decor cluttering the halls. But one thing is glaringly clear—it's all *fake*.

When my father was alive, he prided himself on many things. Authenticity was at the top of the list. In everything he did and with every trophy he collected, he made sure it had the official Baranova seal of approval. That seal holds more weight than gold, so I've been led to believe. It's why our reputation precedes us. We're an old name in an old city with a penchant for tradition.

I've been staring at priceless objects my entire life, so I know a fake when I see one. Most of the paintings and decor around *this* house are well-made, still pretty and distinguished, but *fake*.

My grandmother should have been able to spot the difference when furnishing the place, so I know she didn't have a hand in this, much to my surprise. I'd have expected her to be running the house until the duty was passed on to me.

The truth is far more alarming.

I stare at a framed portrait of a balding man, his whitened smile broad, thick mustache curled, huge forehead shiny, as he stands in front of the very house I'm currently occupying. In the picture, he shakes hands with no one other than my father, former *pakhan* of our Bratva, Tolkotsky Baranova.

My father wouldn't have funded and furnished a place like this, nor would my grandmother, my mother, or anyone in the long line of Baranovas who have claimed this city. They wouldn't make a cheap replica of our own home. My father even looks *bored* in the picture, like he's wasting his time being there.

But appearances matter, and it's the reason my father took time out of his day to congratulate the owner on this once-new manor. It's the same reason why Andrei dragged me to that party last week. Line the pockets of influential people, show your support, and you'll have them eating out of the palm of your hand, ready to do your bidding at a moment's notice.

Like a well-fed dog looking after its master.

This place has the appearance of finery, but it's fraudulent and cheap.

Much like the man who owns it.

"Miss Baranova!"

My head snaps up at my name being called. I curse at myself for getting sidetracked, then I throw in an extra one at Riot for failing to inform me we had a visitor.

"Mr. Mayor," I greet, putting on my best smile. "How lovely to see you again."

He twirls his mustache between his fingers as he enters the room—*his office*—a curious gleam in his eye as he catches me standing behind his desk, *clearly* rifling through its drawers.

I clench my jaw to keep from glaring at my personal bodyguard.

"I'm afraid you'll find those documents quite boring," the mayor continues, meandering closer at a snail's pace. "Contracts and the like. A bunch of legal jargon I can't even read properly without the help of my lawyer." He comes up beside me and closes the bottom drawer with a hard snap. "I'm sure that's not what you're looking for, anyhow."

In truth, I was looking for more dirt on Liam's operations, or anything mentioning my grandmother's name or my father's. But the mayor is right—I didn't find anything the least bit useful in his desk.

Those types of documents must be locked up somewhere else.

Henry Mastiff, affectionately known throughout the city as Mr. Mayor, smiles at me. But much like everything else in this room, it reeks of inauthenticity. "Tell me, do you still go by Miss Baranova, or should I be referring to you as Mrs. Dolohov now?" He shakes his head. "A bit strange to marry backward, don't you think? Tying yourself to your grand-mother's lineage? But I suppose I can't fault you if it's for love. He does seem to dote on you, although I said the same about Mr. Leonov when I saw you two together." His eyes bore into mine. "Moving rather quickly from one man to the next, aren't you?"

My face flames as embarrassment latches onto anger, both flashing hotly through my veins. I've yet to face any scrutiny for my situation aside from my own, and the mayor's thinly veiled censure is a reminder of what awaits me outside these doors. Once the public catches on that I've switched partners from Andrei to Liam, it'll spread like wildfire, and the rumors of how *I* spread my legs for multiple men will be the juiciest gossip in the city.

I'm used to blending in with the wallpaper, not being thrust into the center of a crowded room for all to witness and pass judgement. The difference is jarring, but expected by now. Onlookers want to watch me stumble so they can gossip about each wrong move I make as the new wife to the *pakhan*. It means that I can't let them see any flaws—least of all that I'm being forced into a spotlight I don't want—so I'll walk straight into the damned thing myself. I'll control the narrative before it spins.

It's best that observers like Henry Mastiff understand that *now.*

"Be careful with what you say next, Mr. Mastiff, or I might mistake your tone for censure."

Riot takes the initiative to move closer, all two-hundred-something pounds of muscle stepping out from the shadows to stand behind Henry. His arms remain crossed over his broad chest, but I'm sure if he wanted to, he could reach out and crush the older man's skull with his bare hands.

It turns out, I chose the biggest guard in the house, and he gives off insane alpha vibes.

The mayor clearly notices, his body tensing at the sudden realization that he can't move without touching either Riot or me, and neither would end well for him. "Not at all," he says quickly, a bead of sweat collecting on his shiny forehead. "If anyone knows about getting in bed with people in high places to get ahead, why, it's me." He laughs, but it's stilted. "I was the one who approached your father, after all—the man didn't want anything to do with me, at first."

I catch the note of bitterness in his voice. He stares at the framed photo of my father and himself, his smile frozen into place just as well as mine. He's used to staying in character, too.

"Took some convincing, but we managed to build a prosperous relationship by the end of it, I assure you. *Andrei,* on the other hand—" he scoffs—"boy doesn't know how to respect tradition, unlike your Dolohov lad. At least he's keeping in line with our contracts. Leonov would sooner rip his own teeth out than stick to your father's agreements—"

I stare at the mayor as pleasantly as possible, but it's hard when he's glaring at your dead father's picture and digging a groove into the top of his desk with his fingernail. *Agitated* doesn't begin to describe his change in demeanor. It's no wonder the man's never been married; anyone would be crazy to chain themselves to someone holding that much resentment in his blood.

It's probably why Andrei tried to get out of my father's contracts—if they involved the mayor in any way, he probably saw him for what he is. A bitter, old man trying to be something and someone he's not.

"But I convinced your father to back my election, and I've been in office ever since. There's power with you Baranovas, you know. Your entire organization, it's . . ." his forehead pinches as he considers the proper word to use, "interminable, Miss Baranova. Everything about you Bratva folk is carved into the marrow of this city. Nothing will ever remove that mark. *Nothing.*"

My gaze wanders around the room as the mayor speaks, the strange note of reverence in his voice catching on the glint of a gold-plated globe, the impressive four-foot long print of the city skyline at dusk, the shiny brass buttons on the faux antique chaise lounge set. I've seen mirrors of these items in my father's office, and the resemblance of the room throws me off balance. I catch myself on the desk and stare at Henry Mastiff with new eyes.

He doesn't just work with our Bratva, he *worships* it. The idea clicks at the same time he turns to face me, his cheeks ruddied and hazel eyes swimming with a hint of mania. "If there's anything you want, Valentina, anything I could give you . . ." His hand brushes the outside of my arm, and before I can react, Riot intercepts.

The snap of bone as he bends Henry's fingers back too far is followed by a scream.

"Do not touch her," Riot grumbles beneath his mask, "or

I will break off more than your fingers. Nod if you understand."

Henry's eyes are wide in horror, his face sweaty and pale, as he stares at his hand in Riot's grasp.

I wasn't expecting more violence after Liam's unexpected murder two days ago, but here we are again. Nothing speaks to the soul quite like pain does, apparently.

I snap my fingers in front of Henry's face to get his attention. "You may think you have power in this city, Henry, but I promise you, I can bury you so deep that your own mother forgets your name. *That* is what it means to be a Baranova. None of this—" I gesture at all the trinkets around the room, a new level of disgust curling in my chest—"means *shit* to this Bratva or this city. You're a pathetic excuse of a person if you think you can charm your way into my good graces, or into any *actual* power within this city. In fact, I think a little demonstration is in order." I point to the red lounge chair on the other side of the room. "Have a seat, Mr. Mayor."

Riot grabs Henry by the back of the neck and hauls him to the chair, forcing him to sit.

I take my time crossing to the door and turning the lock, making a show of checking that it's secure before spinning around to face our guest. "My father's office is soundproof. I assume that, as a proper replica, yours is, too?"

When Henry doesn't answer, Riot squeezes his fingers, making the older man scream. "Yes! *Yes*, dear god, it's soundproof, I promise."

I pop up onto the desk and cross my ankles, smoothing out my skirt and humming to myself. "That's good to know, Henry. We're going to be here a while. I have a lot of questions about a lot of things, and I'd prefer if we kept this conversation a secret among friends. You understand, of course." I take another look around the room, checking it with fresh eyes. "Are there any cameras in here, Henry? Be honest."

He points out four cameras, tells me how to turn them off, and where to find the hidden monitor to erase the footage from the past hour. Once that's done, I give him a genuine smile. "Thank you for your honesty. Now, let's start with an easy question." I pull a small notepad and metal pen from Henry's belongings. "Where exactly are we within the city, and who knows about this house?"

CHAPTER 7

EZRA

ALTHOUGH THE ELEVATOR to the mayor's penthouse is large enough to fit twenty people, the box is stifling with only the three of us inside. Mikhail is pacing the six-foot mirror at the back, and Andrei's mask of passivity radiates a cold I haven't seen from him since Tolkotsky was alive.

Mikhail's anxiety is too abundant to keep hidden, while Andrei is determined to bottle up his emotions and bury them as deep as possible. The center of the earth wouldn't be deep enough. Mikhail, on the other hand, looks ready to shout from the rooftops if it means finding Valentina.

It's enough to add another painful throb to my constant headache.

As the elevator *dings* with each floor we pass, I thumb the pill bottle in my pocket. My brothers know I keep a stash of uppers for emergencies, but I've been so high up that a crash is coming soon. A *big* one.

Unless I stave it off a little longer.

I pop the cap and mouth two pills, swallowing them dry.

Andrei's mask slips as he frowns, but he doesn't say

anything. Mikhail's the one who shoves my shoulder from behind. "You're gonna kill yourself with those things."

"It is temporary." *Which it is.* I'm only taking them until we find Valentina—then, I'll give it a rest and sleep it off for a week or two. Hopefully, with our woman tucked safely in my arms.

Mikhail scoffs. "She's not gonna like it."

I glance up at the floor level. Two more to go. "She does not need to know."

"She'll notice if you're strung out on some military-grade bullshit. You're like a walking time bomb."

"I am fine."

Andrei's comment is much less patronizing. "Don't pass your limits. Keep a cool head." He rubs the back of his neck, stifling a groan. "Just be careful."

"I am." *Always.*

When one floor remains, we each pull out our guns. We came up with a plan when we first regrouped: Mikhail will block the exit, I'll sweep the perimeter, Andrei will head straight for the heart.

If the mayor's home, he'll wish he wasn't.

I can feel each steady beat of my heart with every passing second. *This is it.* The moment we *finally* get some answers. The past few days have been nothing but chasing rumors and navigating threats to the Bratva—there haven't been enough results for all the effort we've put in. Mikhail with his bribes and deals. Andrei with his negotiating and information-seeking. Me, with my orders for our men to sweep the entire city. I've been along for the hunt, but it hasn't been satisfying enough. Not enough *results.*

We can't raze our own city to the ground if we don't know where our enemies lie. There would be too much innocent blood flowing through the streets.

Now, though, we have *direction.* Now, we have *action.*

The elevator doors slide open. As I step outside, I catch a bulky silhouette in black armor standing in the main room, a gun slung casually over the man's shoulder and a grim set to his mouth.

Our plan falls apart before it begins. I lose sight of our mission and take a step closer to the man—someone I thought we'd lost years ago.

Mikhail curses somewhere behind me, but Andrei flanks me as I advance. My voice catches when I speak, more of a grumble than words. "I thought you were dead."

Thanatos inclines his head. "Maybe you're seeing a ghost, brother." He doesn't look like his name suggests—a god of death—instead, age has blessed him with defined cheekbones, chiseled musculature, and an even sharper gaze in his amber eyes than before.

If he's been away fighting his demons, it looks like he beat them into submission. But every soul within the Bratva knows that our demons are never truly vanquished—they bite at your heels and cackle at you from the dark, taunting you with their presence, until they finally dig their hooks in and start tearing.

We all know the risks when we join the Bratva. Inner demons come with the territory of being a made mafia man. Much like the ink on our skin, our demons brand us, twisting our hearts until there's little man left behind the monster that remains. I've seen it happen to both righteous men and sinister ones—they either drink to keep their demons at bay, or they drown in other abuses. Women. Drugs. Violence. We offer support programs and hold meetings for the ones treading water, but it's a constant battle. Some learn to cope.

Others burn out.

But most men battle demons of the past still haunting them. Wrongs they've witnessed. Crimes they've committed. People they've lost or let down.

What makes Thanatos and his three younger brothers

different from the rest of the Bratva is that their demons are of the flesh. Still breathing. Left unpunished for their sins.

The eldest brother left five years ago to track their demon down. To see Thanatos back within the city walls means he either succeeded . . . or his demon has returned to the city to settle unfinished business.

That puts his brothers in danger. And Thanatos will do *anything* for those boys.

Even return to a Bratva he deserted.

I ignore our plan and approach Thanatos directly. He's armed, but after all we've been through, I know the man won't shoot. Riot gear hugs his body from head to toe— brand new gear, unscuffed and still shiny, barely worn in. If it's his, he hasn't been wearing it long enough to break it in. If it's not, that means he's been hired by someone wealthy.

Like me, Thanatos is best as either a bodyguard or an enforcer. It's why he was my best man five years ago. Put us side by side, and we intimidated the hell out of these streets and kept our people in line. I've managed without him, but I'd be lying if I didn't say his departure hurt us.

But what matters more than our shared history is rescuing Valentina. If Thanatos is here, that means the mayor must be involved in Bratva business.

Thanatos doesn't work with outsiders.

And the Baranova Bratva didn't hire him.

He eyes me cooly as Andrei and I approach. "Your woman is interesting."

Andrei has always been a master at maintaining his composure. It unsettles people when you can stomach watching someone's fingernails get ripped out with needle-nose pliers, and Andrei has a perfect poker face in the interrogation room. I've joked before that he's a Russian sleeper agent, especially since he doesn't remember his parents or his past. He shrugs it off, but I know that's why he craves Valentina so badly.

Aside from me and Mikhail, he's never had a family of his own. Valentina was always meant to become not just the wife of a *pakhan*, but *his* wife. The woman sharing his bed, his heart, and every dream that comes along with it.

At the mention of his missing bride, Andrei's fingers wrap tighter around the grip of his gun, knuckles whitening, as his calm exterior frays at the edges. "Tell me where she is, and I'll keep your punishment light."

Mikhail scoffs, clearly displeased. "For which crime, *pakhan*, the desertion or the kidnapping?"

Thanatos' crimes are stacked high against him; even those two offenses are capital ones. Tolkotsky would have labeled him a traitor, killed him on sight, had a disposal team cut him up into little pieces, and fed him to the dogs. Such was the late *pakhan*'s way. Cross him, and die.

Things were simpler when the old man reigned.

Andrei doesn't want to rule with a bloodied fist. Some things can't be avoided—violence is a language that flows through the Bratva's veins—but he likes to reward as much as punish. Helping us retrieve Valentina will call for a reward that won't be so easy to give.

"I want a full pardon." Thanatos crosses his arms over his broad chest. "Then, we'll talk."

I'm not surprised by the request. The audacity speaks to Thanatos' unwavering confidence; the man always had unshakeable self-belief, like he walks the path of gods. The namesake has always been fitting. I clench my jaw as I force my gun higher and train the barrel at his head. Even though Thanatos is as much of a brother to me as Andrei, I know where my loyalties lie. Not with myself, but with my *pakhan*. "You do not give orders."

Thanatos remains unflinching as he meets my eyes over

the threat of death hanging between us. "If you want your girl back in one piece, I do."

Mikhail growls from behind me. "What have you done to her?"

Raising an eyebrow, Thanatos flicks his gaze between us. "I haven't touched her, if that's what you're implying. She's been kicking up trouble, though, and not everyone likes it. She's more spirited than the *pakhan*'s wife should be, if you ask me. It's going to *keep* her in trouble until someone finally snaps."

"No one asked you for your opinion," Mikhail hisses. "And you're not getting a fucking pardon, you arrogant son of a bitch—"

"A full pardon—" Andrei interjects, stepping too far forward to remain at a safe distance. If Thanatos wants to hurt him, all he'd have to do is reach out and strike with his fist. Andrei remains as unshakeable as Thanatos, drawing himself up to his full height in front of the other man. Unlike Thanatos, Andrei's power doesn't come from his body—it comes from his spirit. "—for all past grievances from this moment forward, granted when you take us to Valentina's location, ensure her safe rescue, *and* return to the Bratva in full, which means—"

"Save the damsel in distress, kill the opposition, keep your runners in check, enforce Bratva code, strong-arm anyone who tries to pull shit, and protect our people at all costs." Thanatos' dark eyes meet mine, and all the years we spent working side by side reflect back at me. "I know how it goes."

Mikhail flanks Andrei's other side, tapping the toe of his shoe angrily against the marbled floor. "You can't be serious, Andrei. He *left*. You know the rules."

"Rules that I have no intention of keeping." Andrei clamps a hand on Mikhail's shoulder. "We shouldn't kill every man who wanders, Mikhail, especially when they return home."

"With gifts," Thanatos says, his scarred upper lip curving into a smirk. "A princess, a map—" He slips his hand into his pocket and produces something tiny. Tossing it to Andrei, he chuckles to himself. "A way *in*, gentleman."

The key in Andrei's hand is made to look antique, but it's not true iron. The black coating crumbles off the tip as Andrei thumbs over it. "What is this for?"

"The mansion." Thanatos reaches into the pouch hooked to his belt and pulls out a folded wad of paper. This, he tosses at Mikhail. "The mayor's secret hideaway, just outside city limits. It's marked in red."

As Mikhail unwinds the map of Baranova territory, I sidle closer to him. The mansion's location is circled in bright red ink, with trails of red leading down city streets. Multiple city blocks are circled in black, the red lines from the mayor's house connecting them all together.

"Oh, and one more thing." This time, Thanatos approaches me with an object in hand. He thrusts it against my chest, knocking my gun arm out of his way to do so. "She wanted you to have this."

It's a scrap of paper with *from the desk of Henry Mastiff* printed at the top, but beneath the vanity mark is an angry set of numbers carved deep within the surface.

I'm up to 99

Ink bleeds through the paper from the back, and I flip it over to read the rest of the message.

he dies at 100

Mikhail's request for Valentina to count her tears has seemed trivial up until this point. The fact that she maintained a count over the past week—that it's *ninety-nine fucking tears* —hits me like a shotgun shell to the chest. The three of us trade objects and come to a unanimous decision within seconds. This shit ends tonight, no matter how much blood spills.

We won't let Valentina count to a hundred.

CHAPTER 8

VALENTINA

THE ONE THING I want more than anything stays hidden in Liam's pants.

I stare at it whenever he isn't looking—imagining the weight of it in my palm, how smooth the sheath is, how sharp the blade. He fiddles with it absentmindedly, taking it out to swing it between his fingertips every half hour, but even with such a small gesture as that, I can tell he isn't familiar with holding one in his hands.

When Mikhail taught me how to handle a knife, he told me that the blade is an extension of yourself—that it's your willpower coming out to play. If you curve your palm around the handle and hold it like it's only ever been *yours,* then it becomes precious . . . and something like that, you'll never drop.

Or so he claims. During our practice, despite my attempts at making the knife feel like *mine,* he still disarmed me four out of five times. But watching Liam with a knife makes it clear that there's a distinction between a man like Mikhail and a man like Liam: my boyfriend holds the knife like a lover, while my ex holds the knife like a tool.

I'm sure they view me in much the same way.

Cold hands grasp my shoulders from behind, and Liam steps into view of my vanity mirror. He rubs tight circles at the tension in my muscles, humming disapprovingly. "Whatever you're frowning about, *zhena*, I'm sure I can fix." He presses a gentle kiss to my cheek before gazing at our reflection. We look just as good as we did at our last public outing together, back in the *before.* His gaze lingers on my lips, taking in the matte *burgundy blush* that I know he likes.

If tonight is about manipulation, I'm striking first.

His mouth lingers against my skin. "Tell me what you want, and it's yours."

A million girls would swoon at such a declaration, but I can see it for what it is: another thinly veiled manipulation tactic. Behind Liam's tender gaze lies a calculating cold that matches the frigidity of his fingers. He's trying to figure out how to win me over.

I've already told him what I need. I think he's stalling on pulling the trigger.

"Is tonight really necessary?" I fiddle with a garnet earring that won't close. "I've already met your parents, and your brother Anton seems a little—" *too fond of me*—"abrasive."

"Tonight isn't only about my family." Liam hooks a finger into a ringlet curl dangling over the back of my neck. "It's about *ours.* A proper union." The curl snags as he wraps his finger around it and tugs. "Much like how we'll be united tonight. Were you going to tell me that your cycle ended, Valentina?" There's a sharp edge to his voice, proving his ire, but I'd feel it even without his words. His fingers burrow into my hair, pulling at each and every strand tucked inside the tight, criss-crossed row of bobby pins at the back.

My scalp stings even as my blood runs cold. My period ended this morning, way earlier than usual—*damned stress fucking with my cycle*—but I tried my best to fake it. I used a tampon despite not needing one, and I even dug my nails into my thigh to draw enough blood to leave a paper trail in the bathroom trash. Maybe he's been digging through the trash or staring at my crotch while I sleep. I wouldn't put either past him.

Either way, he *knows*.

I meet Liam's gaze in the mirror. "No." I have no intention of giving this man any more motivation to get me naked. Informing him of my shortly lived period would add fuel to the fire that I *sorely* want to avoid. But, to save face, I quickly add—"I wanted to surprise you after the party."

Liam's expression softens on a dime. He unwinds his fingers from my hair and massages my scalp. "And I've ruined the surprise. I'm sorry, darling." He runs a hand through his blonde locks and takes a deep breath. "I'm under a lot of pressure, as you undoubtedly know."

I try not to roll my eyes. It wouldn't be stressful if he were equipped for the job.

His voice rumbles across my skin. "A little love from my wife tonight will ease a lot of tension . . . and I've been very patient." Sliding his hand from my head to my shoulders, he resumes massaging my muscles, pressing tender kisses across my skin everywhere he touches.

I hold my breath as I apply the finishing touches to my makeup, careful to play the part of dutiful wife. To hide the way my skin crawls and my stomach churns every time he touches me.

Tonight. If I'm getting the fuck out of here, it has to be tonight.

"It's been seven days," Liam murmurs against the back of my neck, "and they haven't come for you."

I keep my expression as neutral as possible as his eyes flicker to mine. I've been counting so many things lately, but the days have been the hardest, each one signifying something I'm scared to admit—

Either my men have failed to find me, or they decided I wasn't worth the effort, after all.

"Was it worth it, Valentina?"

I snap my blush case shut. "Was what worth it?"

"Giving yourself to them."

A rush of emotion swirls in my chest—all the longing and hope for a future with Andrei, Ezra, and Mikhail mixing with sorrow at their absence. Silence speaks louder than words, and the three of them have been nothing but silent for days. Their inaction proves that they don't want me, after all, even when I was going to give them *everything*.

I picture myself in my wedding dress, and fresh heartache wraps its tendrils tight around my ribs. A blush blooms across my cheeks as embarrassment floods my system. I was going to let them use my body as they wanted, take my name as theirs, keep my throne, run my Bratva, run my *life*.

All because I thought I was in love. Pain lances through me, and I have to grit my teeth to keep tears at bay.

In the end, was it worth it?

I see Ezra wrapped up in tousled sheets, an inked arm thrown over his eyes as he sleeps through the afternoon. Andrei sitting beside me at dinner, a possessive palm on my thigh as he traces promises of our future into my skin. Mikhail's wicked smile as he follows me across the estate, his footfalls echoing behind me as we play a game of cat and mouse, wherein the predator always tastes its prey.

I don't regret a second of it, but I wish I did. My heart aches at how seven—not one or two—but *seven* days have come and gone, and I'm still here. A small, naïve part of me still believes they're coming to rescue me, while the other, louder part believes I made the entire love affair up. It was, after all, only a week or two that we were all together.

As if that could become forever.

I look into Liam's crystal blue eyes and miss Andrei's ocean—all-consuming, unapologetically strong, possessive as it washes over me again and again, claiming me as his.

Liam could never compare to any of them, much as he tries.

"Even if I lived a thousand lifetimes," I finally admit, "I wouldn't change a thing."

Except, maybe, what comes next.

Liam's mouth curls into a scowl so deep that I wouldn't be surprised if it hurt. "You belong to me. You always have. You'd be giving them something you have no *right* to."

I rise from my seat slowly, pulling myself to my full height. A mafia princess doesn't own a single part of herself. Not her name. Or her personality. Least of all, her body. All of it belongs to whichever man happens to be in power at the time, whether that be her father, her brother or her husband.

But unlike a princess, a queen owns every part of herself. She can give pieces away as she pleases in little glimpses as gifts to those she trusts, or in their entirety as she overwhelms those she loves with nothing but *her*.

Liam deserves neither the pieces of me nor the whole, and I'm tired of wasting my time with a lesser man than me.

I turn to face him, delicately cupping his jaw in my palm, and truly *look* at him. All of him—every single line of frustration and desire rippling across his face—and savor the taste of it. Let his frustration fuel my own anger and resentment.

I'm going to need every last drop to break free tonight.

I press my manicured nails into the soft skin of Liam's cheek, admiring the scarlet polish against his skin. The knife is in his pocket, just like it always is, and if I can grab it, I could sink it into the flesh *right here*.

I glance down to check for it, satisfied to catch its outline in his front left pocket, and take note of the growing bulge beneath Liam's belt. If I'm going to strike, it'll need to be while he's distracted.

Tonight's my first chance. My *only* chance. If I fuck this up, he'll lock me up in that concrete prison downstairs, for good this time, and only take me out when he wants to play.

Turning my grip into a softer caress, I force a smile on my lips. "Tonight, I'm yours."

A flicker of uncertainty in Liam's eyes shoots a bolt of nerves through my system. Although his performance as *pakhan* begs otherwise, he's not stupid. I'll need to be careful with how I play this and only strike when he's truly, one thousand percent unguarded. Go straight for the jugular. Or that artery in the thigh. Something irreparable. Something accessible.

I bite my lip, knowing that I could go for a *very specific* piece of him that I can get between my teeth later tonight, but grow nauseous at the thought.

Liam kisses me, smudging my lipstick as he forces his tongue past the seam, and presses me against the vanity, knocking over perfume bottles and skin products in his pursuit to claim my mouth. I cling to his shoulders as my heart kicks into overdrive, panicking that he wants to do this—*to fuck me*—right fucking now. I grab his thigh, my palm skirting the edge of the knife, and he groans deep in his chest.

He mistakes my fumble for the knife as encouragement, my skittering pulse for excitement instead of nerves.

"Later, love, I *promise*." There's an ache in his voice that I can feel in the hard press of his cock against my stomach. "I'll give you everything, *everything*, Valentina, and finally put a baby inside you, make you mine again—" He pulls away, and the liquid fire in his eyes is a promise of pain. He'll take me hard enough to bruise, to ache, to ruin.

To break my heart when my men, the ones I'd choose a thousand times, don't come to my rescue.

I gave my three men every power card I had in my hand. Everything I've learned over the past seven days. Coordinates. A fucking *map* not only to this place but to every single location Liam plans to hit on his crusade to overtake the city. I gave them *Riot*, the one man actually sticking up for me in this fucking nightmare house. I'm more vulnerable than ever, and they haven't fucking rescued me. They haven't even *tried*.

I slip off the vanity and straighten my dress as Liam tries to remove the smudge of lipstick from his lips. The knife is hard to see around the bulge in Liam's pants, but I know it's there. I know I can grab it when the time comes to use it. If Andrei, Ezra, and Mikhail don't arrive in time to save me tonight, I'll have to make good on my word and save myself.

I've counted ninety-nine tears since I woke up in the basement. I won't count any more—even if I have to shove a knife down Liam's throat as the last one falls.

By the time Liam escorts me downstairs and seats me at the dining room table, Riot has returned to his post, hovering near the back of my chair as the remaining dinner guests file into the room. I'd say his timing was planned, but I had absolutely nothing to do with it. I have no clue where he went today, or if he succeeded in finding Andrei and the others. He seemed confident that he could—I didn't bother asking why —so I took him at his word.

I stare into the face shields of every other guard in the room, trying to picture the men hidden behind them. Is the stockier one behind my grandmother Ezra in disguise? The tall, lean one hovering near the door, Mikhail?

Will Andrei walk into the room pretending to be an invited guest, or will he come rushing in, guns blazing?

An icy shiver runs down my spine.

Are they even coming at all?

I clutch my skirts in my hands and stare at my grandmother sitting across the table from me. She's staring, with the tiniest of frowns etched across her lips. I haven't spoken to her in days. There isn't anything to say to her that won't turn vile.

I can taste the poison of what's left unspoken hanging on my tongue, and I swallow the words down with a hearty gulp of wine. Liam catches my eye then, and I give a clumsy smile as he takes his seat.

"Nervous?" His palm finds my knee. "These are our people, Valentina. Our family." He brushes his thumb across my skin. "They'll love you because I do."

The dinner begins with business talk between the men and an appetizer that melts in my mouth. I don't have to speak since no one calls upon me, and I take the time to continue scanning the room for any disturbances.

Nothing is amiss. It appears as if we're having a normal dinner party.

Disappointment weighs heavy on my heart. I want to turn around and look at Riot, put my hands on his shoulders and *shake* him. Did he find my men, or did he give up and come back empty-handed?

"Tell me, Valentina, what are your plans for the orphanage?"

My knife scrapes loudly across my dinner plate. I wasn't expecting to engage in polite conversation. I've been hoping to fall under the radar until it became time to slip away and stab Liam to death in a back room.

Clearing my throat, I set my utensils down. Despite the unexpected call-out, I've prepped for this. When I'm not sitting like a doll in Liam's lap during his war meetings, I'm scouring the reports on Baranova assets—the ones my grandmother poached from Andrei, anyway. I haven't been around for five years, so without asking her or Liam about them directly, I can only guess about their total volume and value, but from my rough estimates, she must have stolen about thirty percent of Bratva assets from under Andrei's nose. It's mostly random patches of vulnerable real estate. The Baranovas have always owned most of the city, so it's no surprise that some of the less valuable pieces went under the radar. Either someone hasn't been paying attention, or Katya snagged some of Andrei's staff, too.

I return the stares of everyone waiting for my response—which happens to be the entire fucking table. *Great.* Anton's stare is the most direct, unwavering and unapologetic, and I find myself missing Mikhail. He used to stare at me like that, too.

"From my estimates, there are over a dozen or more unclaimed children housed there. It would be within our best interests to find them suitable homes until we can renovate the property. There are a few upgrades I'd like to see, and a larger staff for additional supervision and management. Idleness can benefit an individual's creativity, but I'd like to keep them engaged in activities throughout the year to promote socialization and bonding. It's my understanding that my mother used to handle the foster program, and before that, my grandmother would host movie nights. I'd like not only to continue both programs, but to expand upon them. Pair students with families invested in their futures—teach them life skills, like cooking and cleaning and maintaining a budget. Things they'll need once they age out, assuming it comes to that."

For the first time in days, my grandmother clicks her tongue against her teeth. In the relative quiet of people enjoying their dinner, the sound might as well be a gunshot for how *loud* it sounds.

"Those children do not need additional education, Valentina. Your efforts would best be spent elsewhere. Perhaps on raising your own instead of coddling another's forgotten child, hm?"

It's the first mention of an heir that anyone's given since my return, but I'm expecting it. What is a *pakhan*'s wife if not an incubator for more mafia spawn?

But what my grandmother is forgetting is that both Andrei *and* Ezra come from those abandoned children. Although they'd never complain about their upbringing, they had to learn how to survive on their own once they were officially inducted into the Bratva. It's a hard enough life as it is; we shouldn't make it even harder, or we'll lose more people than the orphanage saves. It's a miracle that Andrei and Ezra rose the ranks on their own, to begin with.

"Those children," I begin, borrowing my grandmother's turn of phrase, "become the very foundation that supports our organization, do they not? They deserve more of an education than we give them. They're as much a part of this family as anyone directly born into it."

"They'll work the streets, as they all do once they age out. They won't need more socialization when it comes to collecting protection fees or handling disturbances at our clubs—we use other means than words here, *ditya*." That gains a few chuckles from the peanut gallery, yet my grandmother remains unmoved as she beckons a server over to refill her wine glass. "They'll become part of this Bratva, and that will be honor enough for the likes of them." The *glug-glug* of the wine bottle emptying fills the air, the perfume of her newly filled glass wafting across the table. I crinkle my nose, although it's more from her words than the bitterness of the drink.

She hates the orphans. *Children* that we have a duty to protect, to claim as our own, because their birth families either can't or won't. That doesn't make them *lesser*; it makes them need us even more.

"Are you forgetting that our *pakhan* and his right hand man come from that very home you scorn, *babushka?* What would they say if they heard you—"

My grandmother's eyes sharpen as she holds the glass over her lips. "Your *pakhan* is a Dolohov, Valentina, not trash blown in from the gutter. We are one of the oldest bloodlines, worthy of the throne because we were born for it, not because we *stole* it."

I realize my mistake as the room falls into tense silence. Everyone here sees Liam—*Donovan Dolohov*—as our *pakhan*, not Andrei Leonov, the orphan who somehow impressed my father well enough to be named heir. They're forgetting who Tolkotsky himself *chose* to succeed him, or they're turning a blind eye to it. And for what? To say they have a legitimate claim over the Bratva?

"The only reason the Dolohovs have any claim over this Bratva is because I'm sitting at *this* table, and no one else's." I stare down every person in the room brave enough to meet my gaze. I'm so sick of these veiled political moves. Let's call it as it is, shall we? "Have we shared the story of how I came to be here, yet? Hm? Has anyone heard that one?" I glare at my grandmother as she chokes on her drink, then at my silent husband.

Liam's turned to stone at the head of the table, his gaze fixed not on me, but on *Katya*, like he expects her to save him. Like I'm sure she's done a thousand times by now.

The real puppeteer has never been Liam, no matter if he calls himself Donovan Dolohov or not. It's always been Katya —not Katya *Baranova*, but Katya *Dolohov*. The woman trying to strong-arm her family line back into power.

"Valentina—"

I cut my grandmother off. She's said enough. It's my turn. "I'm sure it's no surprise that the Dolohovs have dipped their fingers into the drug trade, but you may not have heard that they use them on *each other*. I know, I was shocked too at first, but that was only *after* the drugs started to wear off my system." I shake my head, a bitter laugh catching in my throat. "By then, I was already stumbling down the fucking aisle—the *wrong* aisle, mind you—to marry our beloved *pakhan*. Isn't that right, darling?" I kick Liam's foot under the table. "Why don't you tell them how you jabbed a needle into my neck? Or about the *assault*—I know they'll especially love that part."

My grandmother clears her throat and coughs loudly to cover up what I'm saying, and I roll my eyes as she fakes a coughing fit. Her face reddens, then she quickly downs half of her wine. Must have choked on some anger at my outburst.

Serves the bitch right.

I smile broadly at our guests. "So to be clear, the only reason any of the Dolohovs have any shred of power in this city is because my grandmother still bears the Baranova name by marriage, and I happen to have the Baranova name by blood. I'll let you guess which holds more weight in the eyes of the Bratva."

"*Enough*, Valenti—" My grandmother suddenly wheezes, her eyes bulging from their sockets. Her mouth opens and closes mutely, while we wait for her to finish her sentence.

An unexpected rush of fear freezes me in place. "Grandma? What's wrong?"

Her bony fingers scratch at her throat as her face continues to darken, shifting from red to damn near purple. She stands, knocking her chair to the ground, and takes shallow, rattling breaths. Her eyes drift from me to Liam, her expression shifting from panicked surprise to *rage* in a heartbeat.

The man is *smirking* at her.

"I chose this wine especially for you, Katya, as a *thank you* for everything you've done for me." He taps the edge of his glass. "I know how much you love a vintage red. Has a bitter note at the end, doesn't it?" He swirls his glass, but puts it down without taking a sip. "It's like you said, *zhena*. We Dolohovs have a fondness for testing our product, and we've been working on some of our most potent batches for years. This one, I'm particularly fond of."

I unwrap my hand from my own wine glass and swallow on instinct.

Liam rubs my thigh under the table. "Not to worry, love, she's been given a special bottle for the evening. It won't spoil your appetite."

My grandmother continues to cough, a dry, harsh sound that sends goosebumps down my arms and winds knots of dread in my stomach. No one at the table says anything. None of the guards move a muscle, either—not even as my grandmother slams her fists on the table, knocking her wine glass over. The chosen vintage sloshes towards me, bleeding into the white satin tablecloth. It spreads quickly, a burgundy stain that matches the color painted across my lips.

Liam's favorite.

Katya Dolohov-Baranova sways. Time slows to a crawl as her eyes meet mine, and for the briefest moment, all the animosity between us fades away. I see the woman who helped raise me, who sheltered me five years ago when I ran out of that chapel with a broken heart, who helped me get back up on my feet again.

For that one, small moment, my heart breaks.

She takes a final breath, and with it, she claims what little love remains between us. It's as bitter as the poisoned wine spreading across the tablecloth towards me, tainted and harsh and cruel.

When her body slumps onto the table, all that's left in the hollow silence is a vow between witness and sinner.

A vow of silence. A vow of loyalty.

Liam squeezes my thigh tenderly, reminding me of one other promise now sealed in blood.

A vow of *love*.

CHAPTER 9

ANDREI

WHAT MOST PEOPLE don't know about me is that I never once woke up one morning and decided to become *pakhan*. As a child whose parents went missing before the age of five, the idea of planning for anything other than *tomorrow* was completely foreign to me.

Become a leader of one of the most notorious mafia families in the country?

It was never something I set out to do.

Some would say that it makes me complacent. If I never fought for the position, do I truly care about the duties it holds or the people it protects? But the other piece that most people don't know, is that everything changed the moment I met Valentina Baranova.

She was innocent. One hundred percent pure of heart and mind, like freshly fallen powder snow blanketing the city at sunrise. Pristine and shimmering and full of light. Something I'd never seen before—something so beautiful that it was meant to be treasured.

For a while, I was convinced that Valentina was put in my

path to give me a purpose. I'd done well for myself since officially joining the Bratva—Ezra and I were making a name for ourselves with each new task we conquered—but everything was fragmented. Run these drugs for a hot meal tonight. Stake out this office and report back so that you earn your bed for the week. Nothing mattered besides the day-to-day living, and Ezra and I were good at living by the hour.

But when I saw Valentina, a pretty girl in a delicate pink dress hugging the *pakhan* right before my very eyes, I knew not only that I had to have her, but that if I could charm Tolkotsky well enough, he would give her to me.

I was proven right when he made the offer to give me the Bratva and a bride if I continued to impress.

But the jobs required to climb the ladder to the top became dirtier the higher Ezra and I climbed. Drug running turned into retaliation. Stake outs turned into assassinations. Money pick ups turned into laundering schemes.

If I continued down the path as written, when I'd finally become *pakhan* and embrace Valentina, I'd ruin her in the same way the Bratva ruined me. So I decided to change the organization from within, one piece at a time. That way, when I held my darling wife, I wouldn't drip blood on her shiny white shoes or stain her powdered nose.

As I stare at the poisoned wine spreading across the tablecloth towards Valentina, I imagine her soul looking much the same. Satin white, with patches of deep crimson bleeding through, tainting her just like the rest of us. It's hard to say when her innocence was first ruined, but in the end, the timeline doesn't matter.

Now I can hold my wife without fear of damaging her innocence. If she's just as stained as the rest of us, then I will make her shine as brightly at midnight as she did at dawn.

She'll be made of deep obsidian instead of ocean pearls, but she will still be mine, and she will still be just as perfect.

Liam motions for Mikhail, disguised as one of the guards, to remove Katya's body from the table. Mikhail hesitates for a split second before following orders and carrying her out of the room. I'm not sure where he'll take her—we weren't briefed on the poison plan like Liam's true guards likely were —but he'll be back before too long.

Neither of us wants Valentina out of our sight.

Bringing Thanatos into the fold was unexpected, but welcome. He's always worked well with Ezra and earned a name for himself, of his own right. He's one hell of a shot and good at watching others' backs. We'll need his help to get Valentina out of here safely.

But it's the waiting that kills me. Valentina is *right there.* Sitting across the table, directly in front of me. I could scoop her into my arms and carry her out of here. I doubt anyone at the table would make a move to stop me, aside from Liam himself, but it's the guards I'm worried about.

As it stands, they still outnumber us.

That's why Ezra and his team should be taking them out one by one, first with the ones patrolling the grounds, then with the ones inside the building. Once he gives the signal, we'll grab Valentina and get the hell out of here.

One of the staff members removes Katya's place setting, but the stained tablecloth remains an ugly reminder of her sudden death. I don't pity the woman—she was slated to die one way or another—but to drink a poison from the very man you helped rise to power . . .

Karma's one hell of a bitch.

Valentina leans into Liam's side and whispers something in his ear. I'm not close enough to hear it, but seeing her touch another man makes me want to end this entire charade right now.

She's not allowed to touch anyone but us.

Across from me, Thanatos jerks his head ever so slightly to

tell me *no*. If I cause a scene, it'll blow our whole plan to hell, and Valentina could get hurt.

I grit my teeth as Liam presses his lips to my wife's cheek. He smiles at her, and I can see it in his eyes—the genuine affection he has for her. His arm moves beneath the table, and I have no doubt that he's touching her there, too, on her knee or her thigh, or maybe even spreading his fingers across her waist—or *worse*, lifting her skirt to touch what's *mine*—

My fists clench tightly. There's no way in hell I'm letting this man touch *my* woman. Not in front of me. Not behind my back. *Never again.*

Valentina jerks her arm without warning, and I catch a flash of silver as she swings open a switchblade and jabs it deep into Liam's thigh.

She hisses something harsh into his ear, and although I can't catch the words, I can see her twist the knife with a sharp turn of her wrist.

Liam's face turns beet red, and in the next heartbeat, he has Valentina's throat in his hands, *squeezing.*

Thanatos reaches them first, pistol whipping the fuck out of the man and pushing him to the ground. By the time Valentina's free from Liam's grasp and gasping for air, I've already unloaded half a magazine into the remaining guards in the room. It won't stop them because of all the fucking armor they have on, but it will slow them down long enough for me to cover Valentina.

Assaulting the *pakhan* isn't going to win her any points with anyone but us

At the sound of gunfire, Valentina ducks under the table while the remaining dinner guests scramble for the exit. As the mayor tries to push past me, I slam his face into the wall, satisfied with the telltale *crunch* that comes from a broken nose. When he yells, I yearn to put a bullet in his knee and give him something worse to scream about, but sadly, I don't have time.

The two guards in the room that are under our control tackle the ones that aren't, and I drop to my knees to find Valentina.

She's crawling under the table towards Liam, determination in her eyes as she wraps her palm around the switchblade and yanks it free from Liam's thigh. He blindly kicks out at her and misses, kneeing Thanatos instead. The bodyguard quickly presses his forearm against Liam's throat.

Valentina quickly scrabbles closer, shouldering Thanatos as best she can to position herself on top of Liam. She straddles his waist and crushes one of his hands beneath her knee, while Thanatos blocks the other from reaching her.

I expect her to speak to him, to say something cruel and vicious and cutting as her final words to him, but she's *furious* as she jabs the knife into his shoulder.

I understand being pissed off, but anger like that makes you reckless, and now is *not* the time to let her guard down.

It's why she doesn't see the blonde man lunging across Thanatos' back to reach her.

But it's a good thing I do.

I fire off three shots into his back and quickly take his place, wrapping my arms around Valentina from behind and pulling her off of Liam. "*Zhena*, let him go. We need to leave."

Ezra hasn't given the signal yet. We're vulnerable if we stay in the middle of enemy territory.

She fights me like an angry cat, thrashing her arms and legs to try to force me to let her go. I wrap my arms tighter and drag her from the room, my frustration spiking at the sheer fact that she's trying to get away from *me* to go to *him*.

It's fucking unacceptable.

Once we're out of the room and in the hallway, I shoulder open a random door and toss her inside. I slam the door shut behind us and lodge a chair back beneath the handle. It won't last long, but it'll last long enough for what I need to do.

I whip off my face shield and glower at my wife. She's still raving mad, dark hair whipping around her face as she storms towards me. "Let me out," she demands, shoving my chest with both hands. "I'm gonna kill him."

God, she's perfect.

"No." I tear off my gloves and cup her face in my hands, pushing her deeper into the room. She stumbles as I force her backward, but I don't care—I won't let her fall. "You're *mine*, Valentina. You're not going anywhere."

Not without me.

She grabs my wrists and tugs, but it's no use. Even in her anger, she's not strong enough to push me around. "Let me *go*, Andrei, I *need* to kill him—"

I crash my mouth over hers, swallowing her protests. *Fuck* that guy. If she's going to be angry, let it be at me—I want everything from this woman. All of her anger, her outrage, her pain. Every piece of her, I'll claim for myself.

She is *mine*.

I lift her off the ground and slam her back against the wall, growling as she claws at my armor. Fuck *it*, too—I unclasp it with both hands, keeping my lips on Valentina's to keep her quiet. Once the chest piece is off, she tears into my shirt, and I spread my feet apart and buck my hips up into hers. I'm crushing her. I know I am, but neither of us cares as we tear at each other. Her panties rip easily, my belt buckle jangles over my hips, and then I'm buried *deep* inside her heat.

She whimpers against my lips, and I delve my tongue past the seam to taste her. Groaning, I reach under her dress and grasp her hip as I punch into her *hard*, my anger at being ignored for another man making me just as reckless as she was in the dining room.

I dig my heels in and slam our bodies together.

She screams, but I swallow the sound, greedy for every

sound she makes. I screw her *hard* to make sure she knows who she belongs to. Not *Liam*. Not this *fucking* place. Not the fucking Bratva, either. Oh no—fuck her bloodline. Fuck what it demands from her.

I demand every part of her as mine.

Her touch is as rough as mine as she digs her nails into my shoulders and neck, marking me as much as I'm surely marking her, neither of us caring about how it'll look in the morning.

I'm as much hers as she is mine. She can touch however she likes.

She tears her mouth from mine to pant in my ear, moaning when I arch my back and change the angle, hitting a better spot for her, making her moan as she gets even *wetter*, the slap of our flesh meeting filling the room.

"You're mine," I growl into her neck, sucking a mark into her skin. "You've always been fucking *mine*, Valentina. Do you hear me?" I slam her hips over mine fast and hard, and she wraps her arms around my neck, *holding me.*

"Yours," she repeats, moaning perfectly for me. "*God,* Andrei, I'm coming—"

I lick into her mouth to steal the sounds she makes as she clamps around my dick, damn near cutting me in half with how hard her thighs wrap around my waist. It's enough to tip me over the edge. My balls tighten and I come *hard*, my eyes rolling back as I shoot my load deep inside her.

Slowly, I drop us to my knees and hold her in my arms. "*Valentina.*" I press a kiss to her temple, the edge of her eyelids, across her cheek, on the tip of her nose. "I'm sorry it took so long for us to get here, baby, but I'm here. *We're* here. Feel me, baby. I'm right here."

Her hands travel my body, catching each visible patch of skin. It's not much since we're both still clothed, but she runs her fingers over the scratches she put on my neck and across my shoulders, like the red lines prove I'm here more than my cum inside her does.

I can still see a flicker of anger in her eyes, but she hides it well as she brushes her fingers across my jaw and presses the tips to my lips. I kiss them all, every single one.

"I almost thought you'd . . ." She swallows and sweeps her gaze behind me, avoiding my eyes. A blush creeps up her neck. "Decided against it. Saving me, and all." She gives a half-shrug, trying to play off her confession, but her lip trembles *just* slightly.

How could she ever think we'd abandon her?

"*Zhena*, we drove ourselves crazy looking for you. It only took so long because that fucking bitch—" My words come out as a harsh growl that I have to rein in. "We let our guard down and you suffered for it, baby, and I'm sorry. That should have never happened. It *won't* happen ever again. I promise."

She nods, but I can tell she's uncertain. If we let her get kidnapped once, how can she believe that we'll keep her safe the next time someone tries shit? *Fuck*, we messed this up. We thought we had allies and loyalty—we thought no one could take *shit* from us, let alone our fucking woman—but Katya proved us wrong with a flick of her fucking wrist.

Damned woman should rot in hell for eternity.

Valentina's eyes grow distant, and I hold her fucking tighter. She's not running away from me, not even inside her mind. "What is it, baby? Tell me."

Her forehead crinkles as she stares in the distance, away from me. "He killed my grandmother. I wasn't sure that he'd —" She draws a shallow breath. "He killed her for me, Andrei."

I brush my knuckles across the bruises forming on Valentina's neck. Liam may have killed *her* if Thanatos hadn't gotten there in time. Jesus, I need to give the man a raise once all this shit is over.

"Why would he do that for you?"

"Because I asked him to." She wipes at a tear threatening to fall, then looks at the wet streak across her knuckles with a frown. "God, Andrei, he killed her to prove he loved me. That's what I asked him to do. Kill her. I didn't think he'd actually do it, you know? I didn't think he had it in him."

I draw a deep breath. "Love makes us do all kinds of things, Valentina. And love for you?" I shake my head, feeling myself smile. Fuck, am I in love with this woman. "It's the strongest motivator of all. Anyone who falls for you will do anything you ask." When the Bratva falls in love with her, too, she'll have the entire organization eating out of the palm of her hand. It's only a matter of time.

"Anything?"

I nod as I press a kiss to her palm. "Anything, *zhena*." Her emerald eyes harden instantly, and I wish I could swallow my words. "Anything *except* that."

"I need to kill him, Andrei."

"Now isn't the time."

She rolls her eyes and slides off my lap, stepping away from me to straighten her dress. The skirt ruffles around her thighs, and it's tempting to pull her back in for another round. "I already hurt him. Just let me finish the job, and this will all be over."

"I wish it were that simple, *zhena*. I really do."

"*Make* it that simple. You're the goddamn *pakhan*! Your word is law."

"Not in this house." I push myself to my feet, quickly zip up my pants, and buckle my belt. "Not with these people. They aren't loyal, Valentina, not to me."

"All the more reason to kill him."

"That'll start a war."

As she darts for the exit, I jump ahead and barricade the door with my body. She scowls up at me, still fiery as a hellcat. "We're already at war, so let me end it. Right here, right now. Come with me."

My heart yearns to give her what she wants, to follow her into the other room and help her hold a gun to the bastard's temple. He deserves a bullet to the brain, and more importantly, *she* deserves to be the one to pull the trigger.

But his death won't solve our problems. It will only make them worse. I tilt Valentina's chin up to force her eyes on mine. She needs to know why. "Listen to me, Valentina. Right now, Liam is only acting as *pakhan* because he has *you*. If we kill him now, we'll have six more men pop up to take his place. It'll be another war over who will lead the Bratva. And these other men?" I exhale harshly, not enjoying the thought of other men vying for what's mine. "They'll fight to have you, Valentina, because you'll give them the title and the power that comes with it. But they won't *love* you. They'll use you as a hole to fuck and a body to bleed."

Her expression hardens. "That doesn't matter. I'm with *you*. That gives *you* the title. That should be enough."

I brush my thumb across her bottom lip. There's barely any lipstick left, but what remains is smudged outside the lines. She looks well and properly *fucked*, and it takes genuine effort to stay focused. I have to stop touching her, or I'll bend her over a fucking *lamp* just to get my dick back inside her.

"Until we're officially married, we're not legitimized." I run a hand through my hair and tug at the ends to keep myself focused on the conversation, and not on how fuckable my wife looks. "We'll have people contesting our reign left and right. We need to marry, and then the war will die out on its own. Whoever owns you owns the Bratva. That's just how it works."

She lifts her eyes to mine, and something sparks within

their depths. A flash of brilliant green as an idea takes root. Within seconds, it grows into the brightest flame I've ever seen as determination takes hold.

"Then you can't own me, Andrei."

My entire body tenses, and I have to resist the urge to force her back against the wall and rut her senseless again. "You are *mine*—"

She holds up her hand. "I know. I'm yours. I'm not contesting that." She takes a quick breath. "But if I marry you, I'm still a pawn in these stupid pissing contests, because you'll be the one *officially* fucking the Baranova bitch. But it's *my* bloodline. It's *my* name. I'm the one who owns it. Why can't I be the one in charge if it's my name on the fucking Bratva?"

"You don't have a dick, Valentina." The Bratva won't listen to a woman. It's not tradition. I'm fine sharing the throne with her—I *want* her to use her power and rule beside me.

But to try to reign on her own?

Dozens of people will kill her before they let a woman be in charge of the Bratva.

"I don't," she concedes, "but you do. All three of you do, and *I* own you. Don't you get it?" She presses her body against mine and slides her palm up my chest sensually. "The only reason any man will have power is because my bloodline, my name, gives it to them when we marry. But this isn't *your* Bratva. It's mine. I should choose who I marry."

Fury races through my veins. If she thinks she's going to marry someone else—

Valentina smacks her palm over my mouth. "I should choose who I marry, Andrei, and I choose all of you. You, and Ezra, and Mikhail."

I pry her hand from my face and squeeze it tight. "You can't marry three people."

Her lips twitch as she tries not to smile. "Fucking *watch*

me. It's my life, my body, *my* Bratva. I'll marry who I want."
She places her palm on my chest and pats it three times, once
for each of her chosen men. "You. Ezra. Mikhail. Think about
it. The people in this house, and by extension, this Bratva,
won't listen to you because we're not legitimately married. But
when I marry you, all three of you, they'll have to listen to all
of us. All *four* of us."

Four people running a Bratva. There's always been the
pakhan and his advisors, but what she's suggesting is different.
Not just sharing duties and delegation, but sharing the woman
behind it all. The Baranova who gives this Bratva its name.

It's not much different than what we had planned, except
I'd share the title of *pakhan* with Ezra and Mikhail, and we'd
all be recognized as Valentina's husbands in the eyes of the
Bratva instead of only me claiming the title.

Even if we're not recognized within state or federal laws,
that's not the issue.

It's the Bratva we have to reckon with.

Could this actually work?

Valentina pats my chest once more, as though to console
me. "And then, once that's all settled and we recognize that I
actually own my own damn life and choose my own husbands
to rule beside me, we can kill Liam without all this war
nonsense."

A war is inevitable at this point, whether it's against one
man or twenty. The Dolohovs are gunning for the crown by
any means necessary. If word gets out that they killed Katya,
blood will fill the streets within the hour. Not to mention—"I
saw how he looked at you." My lips curve into a frown. "He'll
fight for you, and his family will fight to take over the Bratva.
It's already begun, *zhena*. The first act of war was kidnapping
you, and the second was killing Katya."

All it takes is one little breath, one small moment for her
to process what I'm saying, for me to glimpse a crack in her

armor. To see a hint of something soft and fragile beneath all the talk of war and death. To see the woman I first fell in love with.

"More people are going to die, aren't they?" Her voice is as soft as it was the day I met her, and for that tiniest, tender moment, her innocence returns.

I want to shelter it. Keep it safe and avert her eyes, tell her that *no, no one will die,* but it would be a lie. One she'd see right through.

I resist the urge to step back into the past by cradling Valentina's head in my hands and pulling her into my chest. I hold her as tight as I dare, probably *too* tight, as my heart does this funny little thing, pitter-pattering like it did when I first held her in my arms five years ago. I wish I could save even one tiny glimmer of that version of ourselves, but it's too far gone, and this life far too dark and twisted to keep even a sliver of it alive.

My innocence was lost years ago, and Valentina's slips through our fingers faster each day. Soon, there won't be any part of that shy, fragile princess left.

In her place, will be a Bratva queen.

Our queen.

"Yes, people will die."

She pulls away from me, a pinched frown on her face as she gathers her long, dark curls in her hands and ties them in a twist at the nape of her neck. When she's done, she holds the knot and sighs. "Liam will be the last. Then this nightmare will be over."

I wrap my arms around her waist and kiss her—my woman, my wife, my queen. We don't have much time left alone. This moment was a stolen slip of time, and it's quickly running out. Shouts and gunfire rain down in the distance, and it's only a matter of minutes before someone finds us.

I make her one final vow, pressing the words into her lips. "His life is yours, *zhena*. To take—to save—it's your choice."

Valentina nods, the sheer strength in her emerald eyes taking my breath away. That spark of fury when I first stole her away started a wildfire of emotion, but now, it no longer controls her. She controls her fate—the fate of this Bratva—and the fate of my heart.

CHAPTER 10

MIKHAIL

CARRYING Katya's body has to be the most ridiculous fucking thing I've ever done in my life. I can't *believe* I'm the one stuck with the dead bitch. Out of everyone in the room, fuckface had to pick *me* to haul her ass out of there. I had half a mind to laugh in his face and put a hole in his head right fucking there.

That would have been satisfying as hell.

Instead, I got to watch the ice queen choke on her own spit and face-plant on her dinner plate. What a fucking joke.

I grind my teeth as I haul her dead ass down the hall. She deserves worse than she got.

The other guards give me a wide berth as I walk by them, like they're scared to be near a body. It's not like she's gonna jump out and bite them. All these bitches are *pansies*. None of them would survive a week on our side of the Bratva if they're this green.

Still, I understand the aversion to this corpse in particular, one thousand percent. The bitch is *nasty*, with bloodshot eyes damn near popping out of their sockets and a stank red froth dribbling down her chin.

A wave of nausea rolls down my spine, and I have to swallow a gag. Bodies are *disgusting.* There's a reason I don't handle clean-up—I'm no good with decaying bits and stiff limbs. I pay others to do the dirty work for me. Always have, always will.

If this were *my* rescue mission, I'd toss the bitch onto someone else, run back to the dinner party, snatch Valentina's fine ass out of Liam's lap, and get the hell out of Dodge.

Valentina shouldn't be forced to stay in that room after witnessing her grandmother's death. Everyone talks about the murder *weapon* being the big bad thing that causes nightmares, but no one talks about the murder *scene.* The day I shot my dad, I walked out of that bedroom and never went back. To this day, I haven't stepped foot in that house. I wouldn't be surprised if Valentina took one look at the Baranova dining room back home and backpedaled the hell out of there.

It's hard to watch those we think we love die, and even harder to stay in the room once they've passed. The look on Valentina's face when Katya took her final breaths . . .

I run a hand down my face, but I can't get the image out of my head.

Her grandmother deserved worse, but Valentina deserved better.

That bastard is going to *pay.*

A growl rumbles in my throat as I turn the next corner. What the fuck am I supposed to do with Katya? "Hey," I call out, jerking my chin towards another guard. "Where do I put her?"

I'm already agitated as fuck, but the *tone* from this man— "The furnace is in the basement, dipshit. Fucking pay attention next time—" about sends me over the edge. I'm glad I can't see his face behind the mask because then I'd have to do something about it later.

I'm really fucking stab-happy right now, but I'm saving it for the blonde bastard who made our woman fucking cry.

She better have counted every single fucking tear over the past week, because Liam's getting a jab of the knife for each fucking one. If I have to stab the bastard ninety-nine times, so be it. Even better if Valentina's right there with me, hand in mine as we slide the knife through his flesh over and over and over again.

One hundred cuts or a thousand—it will never be enough. Not really. But I'll do what it takes to give our girl closure.

I glare at *tone-boy* as I walk past. If this house is a replica of our estate, then the basement is three doors down. I pick up the pace. Can't wait to send Katya on an express ticket to hell and wave as her paper-thin snakeskin burns to a fucking crisp.

As I jostle her body to pull open the basement door, gunfire echoes down the hall. I snap my head in its direction, but the other guards around me are quicker to react. They jump into action, barreling towards the sound, guns raised, as they move in one unit.

A small army is headed Andrei's direction, and I'm fucking *here.*

I take one last glance at Katya before tossing her body down the stairs. She's rail-thin, but she still causes a racket as she tumbles. I know I'm supposed to respect the dead and all, but *fuck* her.

"Ezra," I growl into my comms, "where's the fucking signal? Are we clear?" I run after the other guards, lifting my own gun as I mirror their movements. I can't take down six armed men on my own. I could *try*, but the armor will prove a problem on its own, and once they realize I'm shooting at *them* and not the ghost over their shoulder, they'll turn on me.

I'm not dying without ensuring Valentina's way the fuck out of here first.

Ezra's voice is clear enough that I glance behind me to

make sure he's not standing there brooding. "We are *not* clear," he grunts, more gunfire popping through my earpiece as his team accelerates their plans. We no longer have the element of surprise. Time is of the essence. "Where are Andrei and Thanatos?"

"With Valentina." Both men can hear our conversation, but the fact that neither of them are responding makes my stomach churn.

"I will secure exit. You will bring *lisichka* out back door."

"On it." Reaching into a pack attached to my belt, I pull out a flashbang. I hate the fucking things, but it beats stepping over a dismembered arm or bloodied leg to get to our girl. This way, I can run through the fuckers and get to her first.

I lob the thing right in the middle of the six guards and turn away as it goes off. The men who notice it incoming either drop to the ground or jump out of the way in the nick of time. The explosion rattles the walls and breaks a vase, knocking a few men senseless enough that they crumple to the ground.

Brute force isn't my strength, but agility *is*. I run over the motherfuckers and put a pair of bullets in each of their chests. The good news is that whoever bought this gear is a fucking idiot, because they didn't get the good stuff. It's not bullet-proof in the slightest and only meant to ward off stray bricks and bottles lobbed by angry protesters and the like. The *other* good news is that these guards aren't all trained for close-quarters combat, so it's easy to kick their guns away and put a bullet in their guts.

Huh. I guess there is no bad news.

"Andrei, what's going on?" I catch the mayor of Harlin Heights running towards me, and I swing out my arm to clothesline the bastard. He chokes, *such a pretty sound*, and gives me an outraged look, eyes wide as he cradles a purpling nose.

Andrei sure does have a thing for breaking noses.

"Do you know who I am—" He spits blood on my mask —*gross*—so I kick him into the wall and tear the thing off. Fresh air is a godsend, catching on the sweat dripping down the side of my face. "Mr. Mayor," I greet with a sharp grin, "you never told me you had a hard-on for the mafia. We could have inducted you years ago. Given you a proper—" I slam the heel of my boot into his knee—"welcome."

He screams and folds to the floor like folded paper, dramatic and useless.

"But I think you've got a one-way ticket to hell. Send Katya my regards." I bury my pistol in his forehead and enjoy the flash of fear in his eyes as he realizes he chose the wrong side.

Too little, too late.

The *bang* barely registers over the chaos erupting around me. Thankfully, I don't have to clean up *that* mess, so I keep moving, using the downed guards as cushy stepping stones to put a little bounce in my step. I reload before hitting the next hallway.

The dining room is empty, but there's blood on the walls. If Andrei's with Valentina, he might be busy, but Thanatos should prioritize answering over anything else.

"Hey, Than, where's the party?" I duck as someone shoots at me and cup my ear to hear his reply.

Outside.

Ah, so they've been moving quicker than I thought. Valentina must already be on her way past the gates to freedom.

Well, freedom in the form of an armored Hummer waiting for us at the street.

Most guards don't realize I'm not part of their outfit, so I snag an AK from a body and empty a magazine in the unsuspecting fuckers. Normally, I wouldn't kill so indiscriminately, but we're on a time crunch, and I find that after seven long, anxiety-ridden days of stress and zero sleep, the fucks I have to give are infinitesimal.

I run into a handful of Ezra's men on the way out back, and we pick off the stragglers. Within ten minutes, our part of the house is littered with bodies and not much else. A few of our men get shot, but unlike our enemies, they have bullet-proof vests underneath their gear.

We don't waste lives by going cheap.

Andrei's voice clips through the comms, but he's not talking to me, or Ezra, or Thanatos. He's talking to Valentina, and getting louder by the second. *No, wait*—he grunts like he's balls deep inside her sticky sweet heat, and then he growls out a *you're mine*, and I roll my eyes.

Yeah, they're fucking.

"You son of a bitch—" I hiss, slamming my fist against a wall. "She's supposed to be *mine* next—"

"Now is not time," Ezra barks, and I hear a distinct *click,* which means that one of them has cut off their comms.

The bastard's fucking tuning us out while he rails our girl.

"Fucking *bastard*," I growl, pulling out my phone. We installed trackers on each other's phones years ago, and I ping Andrei's location with a few quick taps. He's not *outside*, the fucker; he's distracted by the promise of pussy, hidden way the fuck *inside* the house. He's probably balls deep inside her right this second. "Motherfucker."

But if he's fucking Valentina, that means they must be celebrating Liam's demise. Good riddance. The world's already a better place without him.

I follow Andrei's location deeper into the house and come across a random set of doors. The ping isn't exact, and it takes me a few tries to find a locked room. I bang my fist against it when the handle won't turn. "Hey! We don't have time for this—"

Something scrapes across the floor inside the room, and the door suddenly opens. Valentina's bright green eyes widen once she sees me, and then she's lunging straight for me. "Mikhail!" She wraps her arms tight around my waist before I can hold her off, and one millisecond later, she's smushing her face against my bloodied chest plate, completely oblivious to the sticky, wet smudge on her cheek or insane for not caring in the slightest.

All at once, my ribs are on the verge of collapsing. It takes effort to draw in breath, so once I have one, I *hold* it. Valentina squeezes me as tight as she can, but the bulletproof vest absorbs most of her strength. This weight in my lungs, the painful flicker in my heart—it isn't because she's hurting me. It's because she's finally *safe*.

I exhale heavily over the top of her head and meet Andrei's eyes, giving him the dirtiest fucking glare. He should *not* have prioritized a quickie over safely extracting her from this godforsaken place.

But now she's here, in *my* arms. *I'll* keep her fucking safe.

A wave of warmth washes over me, and I shutter in a breath. "I've got you, *malyshka*. I'm never letting you out of my sight again." I cup her face in my hands and gently wipe away the blood staining her cheek. Her huge, doe eyes glitter like ripples of sunlight across an emerald lake, stealing whatever's left of my heart that doesn't already belong to her. I lift her on her tiptoes to kiss her deep, groaning as every scattered piece of my heart slots into place now that she's where she belongs.

Valentina tastes like the last ray of sunlight before night falls—a gift from today, and a promise for tomorrow. I swipe my tongue into her mouth, eager for more of her warmth.

It doesn't matter that Andrei got the first taste tonight—this moment, wrapped in each other's arms, is all for me. She ran to *me*. After years of keeping women at arm's length, that's not a welcome I'm used to.

It's not one I'll ever forget.

"I'm so proud of you," I murmur against her lips, drawing one between my teeth. "Such a good girl, coming back to us." I'd feared she might flee the city and make a run for her old life, but the hickey staining her neck and the distinct swelling to her very-kissed lips begs otherwise.

She's just as addicted to us as we are to her.

"We need to leave," Andrei interrupts *rudely*, snagging Valentina around the waist and pulling her from me. I scowl at my *pakhan*, but then Valentina reaches out and holds my hand.

It's not holding the woman of my dreams naked in my arms, but it's oddly . . . sweet. Especially when she holds on *tight*. I bring her hand to my lips and flick my tongue between her fingers, enjoying the way her cheeks flush a pretty pink, just for me.

I'm going to devour this woman the first chance I get.

Andrei turns his comms back on while I enjoy the flicker of desire in our woman's eyes. "Ezra, you ready?"

It's Thanatos who answers, the words heavy on his tongue. If I didn't know better, I'd say he just woke up from one hell of a catnap. His words slur, making him hard to read. All I can make out is *Liam* and *problem*.

Andrei's mask shifts back into place as he neutralizes his expression. "Where is he?"

"The bastard's not dead yet?" I crowd closer to Valentina, caging her between Andrei and me. Lifting my gun, I keep it at the ready and swivel my head to take in our surroundings.

A hallway isn't exactly what I'd call *safe*.

Valentina peers up at me, and I have to fight not to meet her gaze. "I stabbed him, just like you taught me."

A heated shiver rolls down my spine, and I have to shut my eyes. It's the worst fucking time, in the worst fucking place, but if I look at Valentina right now, if I see any shred of satisfaction in her eyes about digging that blade into her piece of shit ex-boyfriend, I'm going to fucking lose it. I'll pin her against Andrei and shove my swollen cock so deep inside her pussy that she'll *taste* me on her tongue. I'll fuck her *hard*. Because that's what she deserves.

Such a good fucking girl, stabbing him for me—for *herself*. *Fuck*, that's hot as hell.

I open my eyes just in time to see her shove her tongue into the pocket of her cheek, *fuck me*, as a little crease forms between her eyebrows. "But I didn't get to finish the job."

I flex my arms, but it's no use. I'm rock fucking hard now. "Where'd you get him?"

"The thigh." She props her chin on my chest and kisses the hollow of my throat. "Just like you showed me."

My eyes roll back in my head, and I have to stifle a groan. Andrei will *kill me*—literally, with the next bullet from the fucking gun in his hands—if I so much as *touch* Valentina in the middle of a war zone. It's hypocritical as fuck after how he just screwed her fucking brains out, but he's the *pakhan*. He can break his own rules.

I swallow, and she kisses my Adam's apple. *Fuck me.* Dragging in a breath, I stare into her eyes. At her swollen lips. The two perfect curls stuck to her forehead. The tempting slip of tongue as she swipes her bottom lip.

If I kiss her now, I won't stop. I'll consume every ounce of air in her lungs until she passes out. I'll keep going, tearing into her for the first time, *finally* making her mine.

Exhaling slowly, I try to reign in my instincts. I tell myself that I can't have her now, but I *will* have her soon. The fucking *moment* we get out of this hellhole.

I press a chaste kiss to her forehead. Not only am I horny,

but I'm so fucking proud of her. "You did amazing, love, I promise."

Her smile makes the wait worth it.

The next few seconds are silent as we wait for more info, but our comms remain completely silent. Andrei and I share a glance. I know what he's going to say before he can say it, and I don't agree with it. Ezra can handle himself.

"Take her, Mikhail. Get her out of here."

I clench my jaw. This situation sucks. We're not usually on protection duty. It's much easier to blow the enemy's brains out when you've got nothing to lose.

This time, we have *everything* to lose.

I refuse to let anything happen to Valentina again. "We'd cover her better together. I need you with me."

Andrei's sapphire eyes harden. He can't stay with Valentina *and* go after his best man. It puts them both in more danger. "I can't leave Ezra behind."

I know he can't.

That doesn't mean I won't try to dissuade him, though. "Ezra has Than and an entire assault team at his back. He'll be fine. He's the toughest bastard I know." If anyone can muscle through an untrained army of traitors to the Bratva, it's Ezra. With Than by his side, he should be damn near unstoppable.

"Something's not right," Andrei grits out, teeth clenched. "You heard Thanatos."

Valentina's body stiffens between us. "What's going on? Is Ezra hurt?"

I meet her eyes, and *damn*, do I hate seeing a ripple of worry. "Maybe, love. We're not sure."

She purses her lips, then narrows her eyes at me. "Then what are we standing here for? Let's go get him."

"It's not that simple—"

She pops the snap on my spare holster and claims my Glock for herself. "It *is* that simple. Let's go."

Valentina doesn't have armor. Or a vest. Or *panties*, if the slip of bare thigh beneath my palm is anything to go by. She's not safe here. No one will be aiming for her, but a person's aim only has to be off by a few inches for the damage to be done.

"I'm not losing you." I grab her arm to keep her from slipping free and running into danger. I love the fire in her heart, but it's going to get her killed. "*We're* not losing you."

She glares up at me and juts her chin out, defiant as hell. "We're not losing Ezra, either. You said it yourself: you need Andrei to cover your back, and he's gonna need you to cover his. All three of you need each other. End of discussion."

Andrei wraps his palm around Valentina's throat and curves his spine to rumble in her ear. *Fuck*, it's kind of hot. That pretty pink flush from before darkens, burning scarlet across her cheeks, as a soft whimper catches in her throat. Andrei's other hand grabs her hip, and then their bodies move together in a slow, painful grind.

"Our queen wants us to work together." He licks the shell of her ear. "If she promises to follow orders, to *run* when we tell her to run, then we'll go save Ezra together."

The whole notion of *saving Ezra* is ludicrous. The man is a tank. I've never seen him taken down.

But the way Valentina's pupils blow wide and her breath catches—*fuck*, my cock's never going soft at this rate.

Saving Ezra together, all three of us, doesn't sound so bad, after all. Seeing my girl with a gun is hot as hell, and she's got a fire in her eyes that I can't *wait* to sink my teeth into. Yeah. Let's save the bastard. We can fuck our frustrations out when we get to him. Sit Valentina down on his face as punishment for making her worry.

Valentina whimpers as Andrei's hand travels up her thigh and beneath her dress. "Y-yes. I will. I'll run. I'll listen."

I slide my palm up the inside of Valentina's arm, enjoying

the feel of her soft skin, until I reach her gun hand and read-just her grip. Even though we gave her lessons, her fundamentals are shaky. Experience like tonight will help with that. *Fuck*, I love seeing her hold a deadly weapon. Licking my lips, I savor the flush trailing down her neck and the way her dress rucks higher up her thighs with each rotation of their hips.

Let's save the bastard, then fuck the girl.

Wrapping my palm around hers, I lift her gun to my chest and press the barrel over my heart. Its beat is strong and steady, now that we have our woman back. Her eyes widen as I kiss the cool metal for good luck, then press another to the back of her palm. "Aim straight for the heart, and you'll never miss."

She stumbles at first when we release her but quickly catches herself, staying in stride with us as we cut to the back of the house. All three of us know the layout like the back of our hands, ironically, so it's quick work to make it outside.

The minute we step outside and I recognize what the fuck is going on, ice floods my veins and damn near stops my heart.

Thanatos is lying comatose against a concrete garden statue—some half-naked Greek god, go figure—but it's Ezra on his knees that makes my chest seize. One of Liam's men has Ezra's arms locked behind him and a knee planted on Ezra's spine, the position eerily similar to the one we forced Liam into a few weeks ago, when Ezra beat the shit out of him and we left him to bleed out on the pavement behind our club.

We've walked into a fucking trap, and it's not looking too good for us.

"Hello, boys." Liam's not smiling. I take it he doesn't enjoy violence as much as we do. It's yet another reason why he's not fit for the role of *pakhan*. You have to have a stomach for bloodshed, and Liam's all about letting his little poisons do the dirty work for him.

I spare a glance at Thanatos, hiding my wince. It would have taken a hell of a dose to knock him out, something potent that works fast. His arm spasms violently, and I breathe a sigh of relief that he's not *dead*, just incapacitated.

Much like our man Ezra Reinoff.

"Let's play a game." Liam holds a pistol to Ezra's temple. "After all, I know how much you love games." Even as he addresses all of us, he only has eyes for Valentina. Watching her. Memorizing her. *Breaking* her. He licks his lips as she pales to deathly white.

This is what she was afraid of. That night, in the limo, when she froze up on the way to lure out her stalker. She was scared we would get hurt. That we would die if Liam caught us.

My heart hammers in my chest as leaden dread pumps hard through my veins. This is Valentina's worst nightmare come to life.

At the time, Ezra said that he was hard to kill, that he moves first before his opponent gets the opportunity. But right now, with that glazed look in his eye and a trail of blood down the side of his face, it looks like he underestimated his opponent.

He looks like he's finally about to meet the Reaper he's spent his entire life evading.

Liam digs the gun harder into Ezra's temple. "This one's called Russian roulette. I'm sure you've heard of it." He cocks the gun, slotting a bullet into place. Or not, if the chamber is empty. *Fuck.* There's no way to know if he's bluffing or not.

He pulls the trigger.

All I hear is Valentina's scream.

CHAPTER 11

VALENTINA

"LET GO, love, it's over. He's dead."

Harsh ringing in my ears makes it hard to hear Mikhail's words as he gently pries the handgun from my fingers. The sharp smell of gunpowder hits my nose when I breathe deep. I stumble out of Mikhail's grasp toward Ezra.

Blood seeps into the grass. My heart pounds harder than ever before, pushing adrenaline through my veins. My vision blurs as tears sting my eyes.

In a single heartbeat, everything's changed.

Ezra blinks up at me as I collapse against his chest, falling hard into his lap. He groans, and I instantly try to backpedal once I realize *he's hurt*, but he'll have none of it. He wraps one arm around my waist and hoists me higher up his thighs, forcing me to straddle him.

"I hurt you." Panicked tears pool in the corners of my eyes. Andrei already has his palm pressed tightly over a gunshot wound to Ezra's shoulder, but I still apply my own pressure. "I *shot* you."

His voice rumbles low, his Russian accent thicker than usual on accord of the drugs in his system. "You saved me, *lisichka.*" He buries his face in the column of my throat, scraping coarse stubble across my skin. "I am still here. Feel me. Feel heart beating." He pulls my hand from his shoulder and buries it beneath the collar of his shirt, pressing my palm flat against his chest so that I can feel his heartbeat. But its beat shouldn't be that slow—if anything, he should be *more* concerned than he is. What if he isn't getting enough oxygen in his system—or what if he's so used to being shot, he doesn't realize how serious this one is—or what if—

"*Valentina.* I am fine. Breathe with me."

Together, we breathe deep. So deep that it aches. He nestles his face in the crook of my neck the entire time, mumbling old Russian prayers. Each of them burrows beneath my skin, soft and sweet, just like they did when my mother used to recite them to me when I was a child. Ezra must have heard *me* recite them years ago while he stood outside my bedroom door, acting as my bodyguard. They're prayers of protection and healing, meant not for yourself, but for others. Not once did I ever expect to hear them from *Ezra.*

As he finishes the final one, he presses a tender kiss to my jawline. "You are safe, Valentina Violetta Baranova, no matter how far apart our hearts."

Even when he's the one bleeding, he's worried about *me.* My heart swells with love for this selfless man. He's always protected me over himself. I've always thought it was because his *pakhan* gave the order, but although his protection may have began that way, a bodyguard doesn't *pray* for his charge. They don't storm into enemy territory with a small army at their back for just *anyone.* He makes shrugging off a bullet wound look like it's just another day at the office when I know it hurts like hell. Not only that, he brushed hands with death moments ago.

He did all of that, and probably more than I'll ever know, for *me.*

The gravity of his vow has never felt more significant. I don't know how I ever took this man for granted before. *Ezra.* His name falls from my lips as a whisper. I don't know what to say. Nothing will ever be enough to show him how grateful I am.

Ezra lifts his eyes to mine, and everything that's ever been left unsaid passes between us with that single glance. He doesn't need words. He never has.

When he kisses me with a slow, purposeful press of his lips, I realize that I don't need words, either. Not when it comes to Ezra.

Our perfect moment of solace ends once we pull apart and reality sets back in.

I may have shot Ezra, but I *killed* Liam.

His body lies directly in front of me, fallen to the wayside after I sunk a handful of bullets into his guts. The henchman that held Ezra's arms behind his back is dead, too—Andrei shot him the same exact moment I shot Liam.

I keep staring at Liam, waiting for him to lunge at me. To choke me. Call me a whore. Grab the knife I plunged into his thigh and shove it between my ribs. To kill me, so that no one else can have me.

None of this feels real. Not the fact that Liam is dead—that *Katya* is dead—nor the fact that all of my men and I are alive and together again.

Andrei barks orders to armored guards, and within seconds, they drag away the henchman's body. Before they can move Liam, however, Mikhail holds up his hand to pause their advance. Crouching in front of my ex-boyfriend's corpse, he whistles. "Damn, Valentina, you took what I said earlier to heart. You got him four times, right in the chest. Wait, no, *five* if we count the forearm."

"I'm not counting anymore, Mikhail." Our eyes meet over Ezra's shoulder. "I'm done counting."

His lips twitch into a scowl. "I'm nowhere near done." He unsheathes a hunting knife strapped to his thigh and begins carving into Liam's body, muttering under his breath the entire time. Ezra picks up on what he's saying instantly, and the pair mumbles together in unison, counting in Russian.

I watch as Mikhail rolls Liam onto his back and digs the knife in deep, wherever he can find purchase, all across his body. Despite it being too late to cause the man pain, he makes a show of slicing into him, counting higher and higher until he reaches ninety-nine. Then his gaze flicks over to me. "Your turn."

Ezra releases me as Mikhail slides his hands under my armpits and pulls me into *his* lap. He presses the knife handle into my palm and wraps his hand around mine, securing the weapon in place. "One more, *malyshka*. The last one," he murmurs, kissing the soft spot behind my ear. "It'll feel good, I promise."

I've pictured stabbing Liam a thousand times. Cutting into the artery on his neck, or his thigh, or slicing off his balls one at a time and shoving them down his throat. Grotesque things I never would have imagined before. Things I never would have wanted.

But he hurt me, stole me, assaulted me. He tried to kill my men. He drugged Ezra, poisoned my grandmother, gaslit me for years, and *still* had the audacity to insist he loved me.

What a fucking nightmare.

I grip the knife tight and plunge the blade deep. Its tip is serrated and makes a hideous, wet sound as it carves through Liam's flesh. He can't feel it—but *I* can. Stabbing him in the thigh and thigh in the dining room was quick. A jab of anger as I plunged a switchblade into him. This, however, is slow, deliberate, and somehow . . . *cathartic*.

Mikhail helps me wedge the knife deeper, pushing it in between two of Liam's ribs to hit his heart. I wish it were still beating. I wish I could see the horror in his eyes as the woman he thinks he loves is the one to kill him.

In the end, I claimed his life, but not in the way I wanted. Not in the way I *needed*.

Somehow, Mikhail understands that.

I count the final number in my head while Mikhail murmurs it in my ear. Ezra rumbles it beside us, and even Andrei, watching the gory display from a few feet away, says the number aloud.

One hundred.

We leave the knife in his corpse.

"What happened to—" I pause mid-sentence, wondering if I should even ask about my grandmother's fate once she left the dining room. Knowing how angry my men have been with her, I can only imagine how they defiled her corpse. The kill was stolen from them, but disrespecting the dead woman's corpse is still within reach.

I take a deep breath. I'm done with being left in the dark. I need to know. "What did you do with Katya?"

Mikhail hums idly, appearing nonchalant as he leans back on his palms and tactfully to avoid touching the bloodstained patches of grass. "If you really want to know, I'll tell you."

"How bad is it?"

He shrugs, but a slow smile curves on his lips. "Could have been better in terms of finesse, but it will do for now. We'll have to retrieve her later for proof of her death, of course, but *then* we can properly decide what to do with her."

"Won't we bury her?"

Mikhail lifts an eyebrow. "Does she deserve to be buried?"

I realize that the decision is ours to make. I don't know if she had a preference upon or any legal documentation regarding her disposal upon her death, but even if she did, we don't have to follow them. Mikhail's father wasn't buried. My mother wasn't buried. Why should Katya be honored after the betrayals she committed?

"No," I ultimately decide. "No, she doesn't."

Ezra watches us silently while the medic patches up his shoulder as best they can. He'll need proper treatment from a doctor soon, but for now, stabilization for transport will suffice. They keep asking him triage questions in Russian, which he ignores. Lacing our fingers together, he tugs me back into his lap with his good arm, stealing me from Mikhail. "Tell me, *lisichka*, how do you feel?"

I cup Ezra's jaw and try to stay out of the medic's way. "I should be asking *you* that." In truth, I'm not sure how I feel, or how I *should* feel. All of my emotions jumble together, between the sorrow at losing people I once loved, the security of knowing that they won't harm us ever again, and the relief that we're going to be okay. "I feel . . ." I take a deep breath and assess the turbulence inside my heart. At my core, how do I feel?

The answer comes out on an exhale. "Relieved, more than anything." I scrub my hand across my eyes, expecting tears to rise, but none come. "I'm so relieved that you're alive—that you came to rescue me—that all of you are *here*." I look over Ezra's shoulder to Andrei, who's speaking with the two medics crouched beside Riot. It's strange to see him without his face shield and to find that he's older than I thought, the faintest hint of gray peppering his dark beard, crow's feet crinkling around his eyes. He stares blankly ahead, either from a concussion or from the toxins in his system. "What did you say his name was?" In the blur between Liam's gun firing empty and mine unloading into his chest, one of our people made a run for the unconscious man at the back—the same man I sent to find my men, who followed my orders this past week without question or condemnation. The man I know as *Riot*.

Ezra clumsily tangles his fingers in my hair, pulling the strands as he undoes the loose knot keeping it all together. "He is Thanatos. He will be okay. Drug cannot break him."

The name Riot feels juvenile when compared to the name of a Greek god. I'd told Riot to go to the estate to get into contact with Andrei, but that if they weren't there, to find them at all costs, as soon as possible. He accomplished his mission in spades. "I asked him to find you."

Ezra nods. "He is former member of Bratva. He knows how we work, how we think."

Mikhail rolls his eyes. "He knows how *you* think. But me? I'm still an enigma—a *tired* enigma. Can we leave yet?" He palms at my leg, slowly sliding his hand up my thigh until the cool night air tickles my bare ass. "You deserve so much praise for getting rid of that *mudak*. I'd like to show the depth of my appreciation somewhere a little less . . ." He crinkles his nose. "Bloody. This place reeks." He turns his attention to the medic shining a light in Ezra's eyes. "Is he cleared yet?"

The medic glares at Mikhail. "Like I told Mr. Reinoff, he needs to go to a *hospital*."

"No." Ezra lifts me from his lap and hands me off to Mikhail, then forces himself to his feet. His eyes glaze over until I put my hand in his, and with one strong pull, he lifts me to my feet. "We are finished."

"Mr. Reinoff—"

"We are *leaving*." He cuts the medic a harsh glare. "Take Thanatos and brother to Baranova compound."

The man kneeling beside Riot shares his sharp cheekbones and raven hair. If it weren't for Riot's huge muscles and peppered beard, they could almost pass as twins. Our eyes meet, and the stranger lifts his chin in my direction.

"I thought Riot—*Thanatos*—worked for my grandmother?"

Ezra grunts, following my gaze to where Riot lay unconscious. "No matter what he thinks, he is part of family. Cannot remove Bratva from blood." Sighing, Ezra pulls me against his side and drapes his good arm over my shoulder. "Let us go. Mikhail, bring car around."

Snapping his fingers, Mikhail orders someone else to fetch the car. "You are *not* driving. You can barely stand up! Let Valentina walk on her own, for fuck's sake. You're weighing her down."

Although it's true that Ezra is favoring his left side and leaning on me more than he likely intends, I wrap my arm around his waist and hold on tight. "Get his other side, Mikhail, and stop shouting."

Andrei reaches Ezra first, sliding under Ezra's injured arm with graceful ease. "C'mon, brother, let's get you to bed. You look like shit."

That earns a chuckle from the larger man. "You are missing chest plate. Did Valentina break clasp or did you forget it after fucking wife, hm?" He shakes his head. "Careless, *pakhan*. I cannot protect you all time."

My cheeks flush as I realize not only are they bantering, but they're casually discussing the sex Andrei and I had earlier. Ezra and Mikhail *know*.

"Don't look so shocked, *malyshka*. There's little we don't share." Mikhail, leading our way across the back lawn, tosses me a wink. "Your little tryst earlier was a much needed highlight to an otherwise dreary fucking week."

We weave through the upheaval across the gardens, stepping around overturned cement statues and over numerous masked bodies as we make our way through the back gate and onto the street. The entire area has been cordoned off, leaving a clear path for us. More armed guards swarm the area, but thankfully, we're left alone. We load into the back of an SUV, with Ezra squeezed in the middle between us all. There's enough room to sit apart, but none of us bother, instead taking up the entire back bench as we tangle our limbs together.

Well, as *my men* tangle their limbs around *me*.

Despite how ashen Ezra's complexion is and how often his eyelids flutter closed, he insists on holding me in his lap, banding his arms around my midsection stronger than any seatbelt. Mikhail weaves his ankle around mine and pulls my thighs apart so that he can slip a hand between them. I'm anticipating him teasing my clit, but he seems content to gently stroke my inner thigh while he peers out the window, a pensive look in his eye as we rumble down the city streets. Andrei takes Ezra's other side, cradling my arm across his chest while he kisses each of my knuckle bones, his gaze unfocused as he, too, loses himself in thought.

Now that we're alone, I can see the signs of exhaustion. The dark circles under their eyes. The way their heads hang low. How they don't say a word, or even look at each other.

The desire to curl up between the three of them hits hard, and I picture us sprawled out on the biggest, fluffiest, whitest bed I've ever seen. *Sleeping.* Waking up naked in their arms to a new world where the threat of Liam and Katya doesn't exist sounds fucking perfect.

"Where are we going?" I ask, leaning my head back against Ezra's shoulder.

It's Mikhail who speaks up, flicking his gaze towards me. As we pass orange streetlights, their glow highlights copper flecks in his eyes. He wakes up marginally as my question registers, a small smile playing on his lips. "One of our safe houses. I think you'll like this one."

"You always think she will like your things," Ezra grumbles, resting his chin on my shoulder.

"She *does*," Mikhail huffs, pursing his lips. "My things, especially. I have *taste*, unlike the two of you. You'd put her in some cabin in the woods, I bet, claiming it's *rustic*." His hand travels higher, teasing more sensitive skin than before. An electric buzz settles between my thighs. "I'll give Valentina the kind of views she needs to recover. Something *truly* beautiful —the kind of view that a queen deserves."

I try to imagine what a safe house might look like, but all that comes to mind is a concrete panic room, much like the room in the basement where Liam tore off my dress. I shiver at the memory, and Ezra rumbles a soothing *shhh* in my ear, kissing the curve of my neck.

Andrei remains the voice of reason. "We'll arrive soon enough, then Ezra needs to rest. He may have a concussion."

"Then he needs to stay awake," Mikhail counters, a glimmer sparking in his eye. "I know *just* the thing to keep his eyes open." His fingers travel higher, his knuckles pushing between my folds to brush against my clit, making me gasp. His copper eyes dance as we pass another streetlight, and the quick glimpse of his tongue sliding across his upper lip sends a rush of heat straight to my core.

"We've all missed you, *malyshka*. Isn't that right, boys?"

Andrei's attention drifts back to us, his weight shifting in his seat. He wraps his lips around one of my fingertips and teases it with his tongue. "Mmm. Very much."

An electric *zing* shoots up my spine as Mikhail applies more pressure to my clit, rubbing just hard enough to get my heart pumping. "I—I don't think this counts as *resting*."

How any of us are horny after the clusterfuck that happened tonight is *insane*. Legitimately, it's crazy. *We're* crazy. Sex should be the last thing on our minds. But Andrei's cum keeps me wet, and even if it didn't, the way Mikhail flashes his canines as he slips a finger inside me *definitely* turns me on.

The car rolls to a stop, and he pops his glistening fingertip into his mouth, sucking it clean. "*Mmm*, just as sweet as I remember."

Andrei pushes open the car door and drags me out of Ezra's lap, setting me down on the ground outside. Sand kicks up around my ankles, and a cold ocean breeze blows right through me, whipping my dress across my thighs. I stare out at the dark, endless ocean, ink-black beneath an overcast sky.

The car doors slam once Mikhail and Ezra climb out. Mikhail places his hands on my shoulders and abruptly turns my body away from the crashing ocean waves. "Welcome to my favorite hideaway."

At first, all I see is the ocean, but that's impossible. It roars behind me, stronger than ever as a storm threatens to kick up. I stare at the impossible waves in front of me until I notice their edges—dark pockets of space on either side where they disappear into shadow.

The ocean doesn't have edges. It's endless.

The four of us move closer, my shoes catching on a wooden walkway hidden beneath a layer of sand. As we close in on the mirage, I realize what I'm actually looking at is a wall of glass. The raging ocean behind us reflects perfectly across it, so much so that when I reach out my hand, I expect to feel its icy spray across my skin. Instead, my fingertips press against an equally frigid wall, sending a tremor through my entire body.

"Get us inside before she freezes," Andrei hisses. If he weren't supporting Ezra's weight, I have no doubt either one of them would carry me inside. I catch his eyes in the glass reflection, and I try to smile around my chattering teeth.

"*Shit*, Valentina, hold on." Mikhail curses as he slams his palm on a camouflaged scanner. "Almost there." It takes three separate body scans to open the door, and then I'm ushered inside by three overbearing men. The house is nearly as cold inside as it is outside, and Mikhail quickly adjusts the thermostat and lights a gas fire in the fireplace.

Warmth floods into the room at the first flicker of flame, and I migrate over to the fireplace without pausing to look at our surroundings. I stare into the flames and hold my hands out, desperately waiting for the chill to seep out from my bones.

It isn't until I feel someone's hands on my waist and lips on the back of my neck that my pulse jumps from a frozen crawl back to a steady beat.

"I've missed you, *malyshka*." Mikhail's hands travel lower, beneath the edge of my skirt to touch my skin. He's warm all over, radiating body heat through my dress and into my skin, hotter than any fire. "I've been going crazy thinking about you. We all have."

Even though I can't feel Ezra or Andrei nearby, I have no doubt that they're watching, listening. "I've missed you, too. So much." My heart aches at how much I've missed the three of them. Part of me believed I'd see them again, but another deeper, darker part *didn't*. My throat aches as I swallow a sudden wave of sorrow despite knowing that the feeling of abandonment shouldn't matter anymore. They *are* here. They chose to find me, despite the risks. Despite how much it cost them. Despite how much it *hurt* them.

I draw a breath as Mikhail unzips my dress from behind. The air is still chilled, pebbling my nipples, and I bite my bottom lip as a needy ache blooms deep inside my body, starting in my chest and spreading between my legs, as both my heart and my body crave to be filled.

I need their love. Their touch. Their everything.

As my dress falls to the hardwood floor, I step out and turn around. Andrei's eyes reflect the flames, his gaze burning as he reclines in an armchair a few feet away. Ezra sits back on a couch facing the fireplace, his muscled arms thrown across its back. Both of them have shed most of their clothes, suddenly wearing nothing but matching black boxers and t-shirts. Like Andrei, Ezra's eyes are wide open as he drinks in my body.

Mikhail hums in approval. "That's right, love, keep your

eyes on Ezra. Make sure he stays awake." His thumbs trace circles along my waist as he sucks on my neck, creating a twin hickey beside Andrei's from earlier. Another *zing* goes straight to my clit as he nips with his teeth, making me gasp.

Andrei leans forward, resting his forearms over his knees. "Show us how much you missed us, baby. Let us hear it."

As Mikhail's hands cup my breasts and he flicks his thumbs against my nipples, I can't stop the moan that breaks free. All three of my men groan in unison, and it's one of the sexiest fucking sounds I've ever heard.

"Do that again," Ezra rasps, "and I will stay up all night to hear."

CHAPTER 12

VALENTINA

MIKHAIL HUMS AGAINST MY THROAT, the vibrations sending electric tingles through my body. My nipples tighten, and I catch Andrei licking his lips.

"Suck her tits, Mikhail." He cups the bulge inside his boxers, giving it a squeeze. "She needs more than you're giving her."

"I'm taking my time," Mikhail murmurs, laving his tongue against the fresh bruise on my neck. He hums again, cupping my breasts in his hands and giving them a squeeze. They spill out around his fingers, too heavy for one hand each. His lips brush my ear as he whispers, "I want you dripping down your thighs before I touch you, *malyshka*."

My core clenches around nothing, painfully *empty*, as the ache for more doubles in its intensity. "Please." The word is little more than a pathetic whimper, but Mikhail's entire body shudders.

"*Fuck*, Valentina. *Fuck*." He sucks in a breath. "If you beg for it, baby, you're gonna make *me* come." He clicks his tongue against his teeth. "And I'm not coming until I'm buried inside you, understand?"

I nod, but his attention has shifted to my chest. He lifts my tit, angling my nipple closer to his mouth, and swirls his tongue around its peak. My back arches, giving him better access, and he finally takes me into his mouth, sucking hard enough that my eyes slam shut. *Oh. Holy shit.* His tongue does wicked things with words, but now I realize how dextrous it really is as he plays with me, drawing out my pleasure with measured strokes and scrapes of his teeth. He pops off with a smirk, then switches his attention to the other side, groaning as I dig my nails into his scalp.

My eyes meet Ezra's, and my body flushes hotter as he grips his naked cock over the waistband of his boxers. He rubs his thumb over the swollen tip in slow, steady strokes. His jaw clenches tight, dark eyes narrowed, as he watches our lewd display. On the armchair next to him, Andrei is thrusting slowly into his palm, suddenly completely naked from the waist down.

If you'd told me five years ago that I'd be naked in a room with three men—three men that I *love*—I would have said it's impossible. Bratva brides aren't shared. They're possessions, meant only to please the man holding their leash in his iron-tight fist, and nothing more.

But the way Andrei, Mikhail, and Ezra look at me, touch me, love me . . . I'm more than their possession or plaything. Much more.

Mikhail's attention wanders, the tug of his lips and teeth slowing as he eyes the valley between my breasts . . . and sees the marks Liam's knife left on my skin.

A sudden rush of anxiety cools my desire, backtracking nearly all of the progress we've made towards my pending *O*. I pull his hair in a desperate attempt to get him off of me, but he pays the pain no mind and forces his face between my tits.

I shut my eyes and prepare for the worst. The *ugly* feeling of being marked by another man rears its head, stealing the breath from my lungs. I'm damaged goods. Touched by another. They're not going to want me, after all, not like this—

The flat press of Mikhail's tongue against the lowest scar makes my knees buckle. He grabs my hips and holds me steady, swiping his tongue higher to cover every single shallow scar from the night Liam carved my wedding dress from my body. They've mostly healed, but the skin remains sensitive, especially when Mikhail slides the pointed tip of his tongue against them. "S-stop," I whimper, gripping his shoulders tight. "*Please.*"

He flicks his molten eyes up to mine as he reaches the deepest scar, the *ugliest* one, and presses a tender kiss over it. "These are mine now, Valentina. You can ask me to stop, or beg with the sweetest words, or scream at me all you like. It won't matter, because I won't listen. Not about this." He licks another stripe along the scars to emphasize his point, then stands at his full height. The fire behind us casts a warm glow over his features, accentuating the sharp cut of his jawline, his perfect, high cheekbones, and the seriousness of his gaze. He brushes his fingertips against my cheek, then gently cups my face in his palm. "There are few things in life I treasure, Valentina, but *you* are one of them. The most important one. And the things I treasure, I take care of." He leans in close and sighs against my lips. "Let me take care of your demons, *malyshka*, so that you only have room for me."

My scars itch at the memory of Liam, the demon who carved them.

I wrap my arms around Mikhail's neck and cling to him— to the promise of leaving the pain of my past behind. The past seven days, the past seven years, all of it. The betrayal and heartbreak and death lurking around every corner. I want something new. Something brighter and warmer that glitters in the sunlight like gold.

I want to be treasured.

I want to be *loved*.

"*Please*," I whisper, molding my body against his, feeling his warmth seep into my soul, "take me, Mikhail. I want to be yours—"

He claims my mouth with impatience, his gentle touch turning feral in a heartbeat as he wraps my hair around his fist and steals any chance for air I have. He licks the seam of my lips and groans as he slips past, claiming more of me for himself. "So fucking sweet," he rasps, "begging like that, all for me—"

I'm swept up by his kiss and consumed by his passion, completely at his mercy as he walks me back. My feet touch something soft, and he pulls me to a stop. "Lie down for me, love. Right here." He snags a throw pillow from Ezra's outstretched hand and sets it down on the rug.

Once I'm on my back, Mikhail adds a second pillow to prop me up, giving me a perfect, eye-level view of Ezra and Andrei's fully erect cocks. "Spread your legs, baby," Andrei instructs, spreading his own farther apart as he leans further back in his chair. "I want to see that perfect fucking pussy."

I don't even get a chance to do as I'm told—Mikhail kneels in front of me, grabs my ass to drag me closer, and bends my knees over my chest as far as they'll go, putting me on full display for the room. My flush runs hotter, spreading down my neck, as Mikhail *stares* at my slit and licks his lips.

"She is glistening," Ezra grunts, stroking himself slowly. "Think she is ready for you, brother?"

"Not yet. Hold your legs for me, love." Once I'm hugging my thighs to my chest, he lets go and grabs his cock at the base. A thick vein pulses along the side as he rubs it against me with a slow rock of his hips, then, without warning, he smacks my pussy with it. "You're not dripping down your thighs yet, are you, *malyshka*?"

My core clenches as arousal pulses through me. I'm close, so fucking close. But I shake my head, because *no*, I'm not to the level he wants yet.

His lips curve into a pleased grin. "That's right, you're not there yet. But we both know what you need to get there. We shared a *very* special moment together, don't you remember?" He slides his cock over my slit, spreading my arousal and bumping my clit with the tip.

I cry out as a jolt of pleasure zips through me. *Familiar* pleasure. We've done this before, but with a little more clothing, and a lot more privacy. My eyes widen as he continues rubbing against me, a feral gleam in his eye.

He wants me to finger myself while they all watch.

Slowly, I drag my palm down the back of my thigh and around the front to reach between my thighs. Mikhail graciously takes over, holding my thighs when I can't manage any more. I expect him to move his dick out of the way, but he nudges my entrance as my fingertips swirl over my clit.

My back arches against the pillows as I gasp in a shallow breath. This isn't the same at all—this is *so much better*. I throw my head back and moan as I touch myself, knowing my men are watching, stroking themselves, getting off on this as much as I am.

Mikhail chokes on a growl as I dip my fingers lower and slide one inside, curling it deep before dragging it back out. When I bring my fingers back to my clit, his cock nudges my entrance again, the tip sliding inside.

We moan in unison, and Ezra curses loudly from the couch. "Move your dick, Mikhail, unless you are going to fuck. You are in way of perfect view."

"Fuck off," Mikhail hisses, rocking his hips as he slides only the tip in, then back out, then in again. It's agony to feel the start of the stretch, the heat, only for him to retreat.

I press my fingers harder against my clit, whimpering as Mikhail's hips stutter and he slips another inch inside.

"Goddamn," he grunts, teeth clenched, jaw locked tight. "How are you so tight, baby? I'm gonna have to stretch you out with my fat fucking cock, aren't I?"

I nod frantically. Yes. Anything. "*Please* fuck me, Mikhail. I want your cock inside me." The request is a high-pitched whine. A light sheen of sweat breaks out across my skin as my need spikes and I near my breaking point.

Mikhail thrusts harder, passing over my slit to grind against my clit, forcing a cry past my lips. "I need you to come first, baby, for your pussy to clench so tight that your cum leaks out. Can you do that for me?"

Andrei appears by my side, holding his cock over my chest. A vein beneath the head throbs as he thumbs it. "For us, *zhena*. Come for us, and we'll come for you." Ezra appears a moment later on my other side, kneeling with a pained grunt. He fists his cock over my face, hovering just high enough that I can't reach it. His tattooed fingers glide over his length with ease, and I wish he would lower it into my mouth. I want to feel his cock pulse on my tongue when he comes.

Once Andrei kneels, he grabs my tit and pinches my nipple between his knuckles, spitting on it so that there's more pleasure than pain. The three of them watch as my body twitches beneath their heated gazes, their focus zeroing in on my pussy when my moans go silent and my eyes screw shut.

I come so hard that my world collapses into a single point of white-hot pleasure. The air in my lungs gets trapped, my mind momentarily frozen, and all I can do is *feel*. The plush carpet at my back. The bruising grip on my thighs. The hot streaks of cum striping my chest and neck.

Ezra and Andrei kept their promise, coming when I did. Now, it's Mikhail's turn.

He waits until my vision clears, his cock twitching against

my hole. "Dripping wet, baby. Just like I need." He drags his cock through my folds, spreading my arousal over his shaft, and groans. "You're fucking perfect, Valentina, so perfect for me." He lifts his hips and presses the tip past my lips, leaning harder on the back of my thighs, pinning me down. He goes slow despite how wet I am, forcing himself to savor the feel of my pussy fluttering around him.

The smell of sex hovers in the air around us, overpowering the smoke from the fireplace, and I drag in a needy breath as Mikhail slides another inch inside and Ezra rubs his cock on my chest, *still hard* despite the cum and the concussion. Andrei grabs my thigh and pulls it farther out, giving Mikhail better access. "Fill her sweet pussy up, brother. She'll come again when you do."

Mikhail exhales harshly, his eyes flashing. "She fucking better." With a hard thrust, he slams the rest of the way home. Rapid-fire Russian flies past his lips as he fucks me *hard*, pounding our hips together relentlessly, forcing me to take it. I can't catch my breath, barely stealing a sliver of air when he bottoms out and hits something *deep*, sending shockwaves through my body.

I want to watch Mikhail while he fucks me. I want to see him come undone as he comes, the way his chest muscles will twitch and ripple, the way he'll arch his back to go *deeper*, to come harder, to fill me up the way we've both always wanted.

But it's Ezra's eyes that claim mine, finally focused past the haze of drugs, as he stares at my face. If I weren't already flushed crimson, his gaze would burn me from the inside out. Unparalleled *need* radiates in those midnight eyes, the press of his erection on my collarbone insistent, yet compared to the way Mikhail digs in his heels and *grinds* his cock deep in my pussy, somehow *tender*. I pant hot puffs of air in his direction, somehow managing to snake my arm up his thigh and grab his hand. I twine our fingers together and squeeze, tugging him closer.

Understanding ripples across his face, and he cups the back of my head to draw my mouth to his length. "Is this what you want, *lisichka*? Hm?" I flick my tongue against his weeping slit, and he groans as he pushes the tip past my lips. Salt hits my tongue, and I suck greedily, swallowing as much as I can. "*Fuck*, Valentina, *fuck.*"

Mikhail echoes the sentiment, slowing his pace to drag against my inner walls and draw the moment out. "Fuck, *malyshka*, you're fucking breathtaking, you know that? *God*, I'm gonna come so hard—" His voice breaks as he buries himself deep, his cock twitching with each pulse of his release, hot and wet and *delicious*—

With a groan, Ezra holds my head down, burying himself in the back of my throat as he comes again. Tears fill my eyes as I swallow him down, needing air, but unwilling to let him go. He pulls his cock out slowly on an exhale, leaning over me to press a kiss to my forehead. "You are best medicine," he rumbles, nosing my temple. "Beautiful fox."

I hold Ezra's hand tight, then reach out with my other one for Mikhail. He grabs it fast and holds on tight, still thrusting his hips in a gentle glide, as unwilling to let me go as I am with him.

"I love you." I squeeze both of their hands, looking between the two of them, then at Andrei. *They came for me.* Not just here, in this sex-filled room, but they came to save me. "You could have left me behind, but you didn't." I bite my bottom lip hard as emotion threatens to spill over. Damn it. A queen shouldn't cry. I shouldn't get all weepy about this.

But I'm *touched*. They risked their lives to pull me out of that hell. "Thank you."

Andrei kisses my calf before lowering it back down to the

floor. "*Zhena*, darling, we would follow you to the ends of the earth if it meant bringing you back."

"To heaven or hell," Ezra murmurs, pressing a kiss to the back of my hand. "We would break through gates for you."

Mikhail rubs his palms down my thighs as he eases my legs to the ground. There's a pinch between his eyebrows that shouldn't be there after coming so hard inside me. "Don't you get it yet?" He crawls over my body until we're eye to eye with each other. I bite my bottom lip until he sweeps in and steals a kiss, melting against my lips. There's a soft edge to the kiss that's new for us, filling my heart with warmth. My name falls from his lips in a hushed whisper. "Valentina. My love. My treasure."

"*Moya zhena.*"

"*Lisichka.*"

I open my eyes to find them all staring at me with the same tenderness that I feel, reflecting it right back at me. Mikhail cups my cheek and smiles so fucking beautifully that I can't breathe.

"I'm in love with you, *malyshka*, so fucking in love with you." He kisses me deep, forgetting how to be gentle as he pulls me under his spell and wraps me in his arms, slipping back inside my molten core just as easily as he's slipped inside my heart.

We fall into a rhythm, all three of us nowhere near finished now that we're back together, consumed by each other, lost to the world, needing only ourselves to survive.

This is home. It's always been home.

CHAPTER 13

VALENTINA

I AWAKE to the lingering scent of sex and cigarette smoke hanging in the air, a tail of the latter curling over my head. I tug my right arm free from whoever's clutching it to their chest—Mikhail, it turns out—and slide my left leg free from between Andrei's thighs. Both are sound asleep and lightly snoring against the patter of rain pelting the floor-to-ceiling windows.

The instant we moved to the master suite and landed on the bed, Mikhail passed out. Right behind him was Andrei, managing to land with his head on a pillow, at least, which left Ezra and me to find room for ourselves somewhere in between. I slipped unconscious within minutes, the soothing drag of Ezra's fingers through my hair lulling me into a deep sleep.

I reach for him around the tangle of body parts and bedsheets, squinting in the dark when I don't feel him. "Ezra?" My heartbeat jumps as I check the floor for his body, but thankfully, the hardwood's empty. He didn't fall out of bed, meaning he's lingering nearby.

When lightning flashes, I follow the trail of smoke until I

catch a faint, orange glow beside the bay window. Ezra takes a drag of his cigarette, holding the smoke in his lungs. I'm not sure he realizes I'm awake until he speaks.

"You should be sleeping." He exhales slowly, blowing smoke in my direction. "Close eyes, *lisichka*. I am not far."

I tug a throw blanket free from beneath Mikhail's thigh. Draping it over my shoulders, I scoot to the edge of the bed and quickly cross the room to Ezra. "You must be freezing over here." The hardwood is damn near frozen beneath the soles of my feet, making me shiver as a draft breezes up my bare legs. "Come back to bed with me."

He hooks an arm around my waist and pulls me into his lap. "I am not tired." The loveseat is made for two average-sized people, not a mountain and his lover. Between his muscled thighs and my thick ones, we easily fill the entire seat. I loop my arms around his neck and drape the blanket over both of us, cocooning us in whatever warmth's left. It's not much, but it's enough that Ezra makes a pleased sound in the back of his throat.

"Why can't you sleep? Are you in pain?" The question feels stupid after everything we've been through tonight, but it still feels important to ask. There could be any number of things running through his head, and I want to know which knot I need to pull loose to get him back to bed, *asleep,* instead of staring at the ceiling all night.

He runs his fingers idly through my curls, separating tangles and splitting ringlets until his hand combs through smooth. Smoke billows around us as he breathes deep and exhales slowly. "I am . . ." A crack of thunder fills the room, the bright white strike of lightning flashing in his eyes. "On medication. It makes sleep difficult to find."

I didn't know he'd been prescribed anything, but then again, it's never come up before and I hadn't thought to ask.

"Is insomnia a side effect, then? Have you tried melatonin? What does your doctor say?"

He snorts around the cigarette pinched between his teeth. "Not that type medicine. This is only for emergency." He sighs, resting his head on the glass pane behind him. Another crack of thunder sounds before he continues. "I do not sleep, Valentina." He exhales slowly as he continues playing with my hair. "Sleep makes you target. It makes you sloppy. You cannot die if you are not tired, not off guard." Ashes fall from the tip of his cigarette, burning out before they touch our blanket. "So, I take the pills. I do not sleep. I keep watch so that my *pakhan* and *zhena* can sleep. They do not worry, because I am here. I am awake, so they are not."

The weight of his words steals the breath from my lungs. "How long have you been awake, Ezra?"

He loops his fingers around what few curls have survived his touch. "Few days."

My eyes narrow as he continues avoiding the question. "How many?"

With a noncommittal shrug, he taps his cigarette to the side and drops ashes on the hardwood. "A few."

I scrub my aching eyelids. I didn't get enough sleep for this conversation. *He* hasn't gotten any sleep in God knows how long. "You need to sleep, Ezra. You can't run on drugs and testosterone all the time. I want my husband to be *whole*, which means eating healthy, whole grains and getting a full eight hours of sleep each night. Okay?"

He takes another drag. "Andrei does not get eight hours sleep."

"I wasn't talking about him."

That gets Ezra's attention. He perks up in a heartbeat, shifting his weight as he sits up straighter. "You either have crazy plan or you have big problem. Andrei will not let you marry other man. He is in love with you."

This is the first time I've heard someone speak so casually about what Andrei and I have, and it fills my heart with light. I lean into Ezra for a kiss when he suddenly grimaces. My heart jumps to my throat and I pull back immediately, being careful not to put any weight on his torso. "Oh, shit, did I touch your —" The words *bullet wound* sour on my tongue—"um, bandage?"

Ezra holds his breath as he takes my wrists in his hands. The woven blanket falls off my shoulders and pools around our thighs, blasting us with cold air. His eyes dip to my chest and take in my naked body, sending a wave of heat through my bloodstream. Thumbing my wrists, he lifts one to his lips and presses a kiss to my pulse point. "You can touch me any place, *lisichka*. I feel no pain with you."

Bold-face lies, but sweet ones.

I lean in, more careful to avoid his injury this time, and press a gentle kiss to his lips. "You took a bullet for me. I never said thank you."

When I retreat farther back to give him space, he doesn't let me, surging forward and stealing another kiss, then another, and another, until I'm breathless and aching.

His voice rumbles across my lips, promising more. "I do not want *thanks*." Surprisingly gentle, he molds his mouth over mine, insistent but patient.

My heart skips a beat. "What do you want?"

His stubble scratches my cheek as he wraps the blanket back over my shoulders. I shiver as my body welcomes the extra layer, while Ezra hums in the back of his throat and slides his palms down the outside of my arms, rubbing warmth into my skin with slow, methodical movements. The answer shines in his onyx eyes, lingers in his gentle touch.

His lips hover over mine, and my heart seeks his. Aching. Wanting. *Needing.* He exists in every cavern of my heart, pumping through my bloodstream. This man loves me. I know it.

But he doesn't *say* it.

His lips brush over my jaw as he travels lower, setting into the curve of my neck. He sighs, a weariness weighing him down. "You must marry Andrei."

I clutch Ezra tightly in my arms, cradling the back of his head and scraping my nails against his scalp. *He loves me.* But it's not easy for him. It never has been.

"You must marry Andrei," he repeats, pressing an open-mouthed kiss to my skin, searing it with heat. "He is *pakhan*, and you are princess. It is my job to keep promise—to *protect*. I will take bullet for you, Valentina—I will take beating and broken bone, poison and pain, to keep you safe. That is promise for you, Princess."

I press my palm over his heart, feeling its beat stutter and skip, *erratic*, and overwhelming sadness washes over me. He would take on every danger coming our way, to keep me safe. "You would die for me."

Ezra's lips travel the expanse of my neck, a trail of fire that ignites my blood. I gasp as he nips my skin and groans, palming my ass to pull me deeper into his lap.

"E-Ezra." I bite my lip and stifle a moan, the bulge beneath me *very* large and growing by the second.

His free hand slides up the back of my neck and into my hair, pulling me impossibly close. I can't tell where I end and he begins.

"I cannot make promise of future," he rasps, sucking a bruise onto my neck, "I cannot speak pretty lies, Valentina. My life is Bratva. I live for princess. I die for queen. Title does not matter, I do not exist without her." He lifts his hooded eyes to mine, his words soft and slow. "I can not exist without *you*."

I crash into him like a wave against the shore, claiming his *stupid, romantic, Russian* mouth with mine, then overpowering him as the rest of my body surges over his. I climb deeper into his lap and scrape my nails through his hair; the *sound* he makes curls my toes. He matches my ferocity as he licks into my mouth and slides his palms over my hips, my stomach, up my ribs, over my breasts, into my hair, pulling me harder into him, like he can't get enough, like he *needs* every part of me on offer. "Valentina," he sighs, throwing his head back when I grind down hard with a slow rotation of my hips. He makes a choked sound as he bucks up into me, matching my movements. "*Valentina*," he hisses, grabbing my ass *hard* and as he takes over, rubbing my lips over his length, soaking his boxers and damn near forcing himself in. "Naughty fox, rubbing dirty cunt all over. Your pussy is used. Full of cum." He thrusts, applying pressure to my clit and making me gasp. "Are you ready for more, *lisichka*?"

He picks me up as he stands in one swift motion, carrying me out of the bedroom and down the hall to another guest room. I'm kissing his neck when he tosses me onto the bed and strips, his cock springing free before he's even pulled his shirt over his head. While he's tossing his shirt to the floor, I'm scooting up the bed and throwing my legs open in welcome.

Lightning flashes, painting his body white. In an instant, man transforms to marble, the picture of Adonis as he crawls on top of me and slots himself between my thighs. Our lips meet the same moment as our hips, both of us groaning as our bodies merge into one. Ezra grips the headboard overhead and surges harder, lifting my knee to drive himself deeper. My pussy clenches, already gushing wet from Mikhail's release and my own mixing together, and now *Ezra* is determined to make an even bigger mess of me.

"*Ohhhh.*" Shit. That's hot. That's *really* fucking hot.

His smile is pure, confident *sex* that I'd expect more from Mikhail, but catching the satisfied glimmer in Ezra's dark eyes

damn near tips me over the edge. I toss my head back into the
pillow with a longer, louder moan.

"Perfect, *lisichka*, *perfect*. Beautiful woman. Taking cock
so well." He tilts his hips and his cock drags against my walls as
the angle shifts, making me whine. He grunts with every other
thrust, slamming the headboard into the wall in a steady *bam
—bam—bam*. Leaning in, he captures my lips in a kiss. "I fill
you up so good, remember? I make you feel good. Say it."

I mumble something incoherent, and he smacks my thigh.
"*Say it*."

"You make me feel good!" The flash of pain jolts through
my body, ramping up the liquid-hot feeling inside me. "*Fuck*,
Ezra, you make me feel *so* good. So fucking good. You fill me
up *so well*."

"Better than others," he rumbles, sucking on my bottom
lip with a tenderness that catches me off guard. "I fit you *best*,
yes?"

The man is fishing for compliments while he rearranges
my guts. *Ridiculous.* But another hard thrust has me nodding
along to anything he says. "Y-yes, so much better. Yes."

Ezra hums his approval as he slows the pace, leaning back
to take in my entire body, both of us bathed in silver moon-
light. I feel like a sweaty mess, flushed and overheated, panting
and restless with a need for release. He sees it all, and *still* he
looks at me like I'm the most beautiful creature in the world.
My heart clenches tight in my chest.

His expression breaks as he comes, the confidence fading
for something much more tender, much more *real*. He cups
my cheek in his palm and presses a sweet kiss to my lips, licking
leisurely inside my mouth as his cock pulses heat deep inside
me, painting my walls in a sticky-sweet promise. It's not the
way he fucks me that makes me come—it's the way he *holds*
me once it's over, this mountain of a man who could crush me
in an instant, hovering in place, being careful not to rest too

much weight on me when it's clear that's all he wants. To bury me against his chest and hide me away from the others, even if just for tonight. To steal a sweet moment for ourselves. A moment that was, in the past, *impossible.*

I slide my palms up and down Ezra's back, careful to avoid the exit bullet wound over his shoulder, and enjoy the way he *purrs* from the attention. Slowly, gently, he lowers himself on top of me. His voice slurs as he tells me the secrets of his heart —how much he loves me, how grateful he is that I'm safe, and how fucking good it feels to be in someone else's arms.

I hold him close as he falls asleep in fits, his body fighting the drugs lingering in his system and the new rush of oxytocin from the sex. I *shhh* when he twitches awake, scratch his head and back until he relaxes, and snuggle close when his breathing slows.

Finally, my mountain falls asleep.

CHAPTER 14

VALENTINA

As a clatter from outside of our bedroom stirs me from slumber, Ezra bands his arm tighter around my waist and buries me beneath his naked chest, burrowing us both deeper into the blankets like he's a bear preparing for winter slumber. My heart melts as he snuggles close, but the rest of me literally *melts*. Turns out that Ezra is merely masquerading as human; he's really a furnace made of scorching hot muscles and testosterone, and I'm *dying*. I wriggle around until I find a blessed opening in the covers and snag a brisk lungful of cool air. "Ezra," I wheeze, struggling to detach myself from the bear. "Too hot. Melting. *Dying*."

He loosens his grip so I can scoot a few inches away, but right as I'm about to escape, he latches onto my hips and pulls me back. "Sleep," he mumbles, voice rasping with fatigue. "*Shhh*." With a grunt, he wedges my thigh between his and holds me in place. "*Lisichka. Mmm.* You are warm." Slowly, he drags his stiff cock against my naked thigh, burning a brand into my skin.

I gasp for air as an inferno courses through my veins. My pussy throbs, despite the punishment she endured last night, and a whine catches in my throat. "I can't, Ezra, *please*. I'm dying. It's too hot. I will die if you so much as *think* about putting that thing inside me. Stop it."

He grunts as I detangle my arms from the sheets and finally get a glorious burst of cool air against my flushed skin. Last night, the house was ice cold, but now that four bodies and a warm fire have invaded the premises and burrowed in for God knows how long, the temp has improved from frigid tundra to chilled mountain morning. Bright sunlight streams through the gossamer curtains. Is it morning? Afternoon? When exactly did we fall asleep last night?

The blankets shift beside me as Ezra reveals his face to the sunlight. "If they know you are awake, they will steal you away." He slowly pries his eyes open, maintaining a stony expression despite the tousled hair and lingering imprint of the pillowcase on his cheek. His hands wander up and down my thigh as he holds it in place against his length. "I am not ready to give you back."

A rush of heat as he continues the slow grind into my thigh makes my body flush hotter. I can still feel both Ezra's and Mikhail's cum inside me, slicking my thighs every time I dare move them. I never had a chance to clean up before falling asleep last night. Surely Ezra won't want to go for another round when I'm already so . . . *full*. Besides, we're all forgetting the most important fact in the face of our horny: Ezra's *injured*. "You need to rest." As I attempt to slip from his grasp, he grumbles dissent and drags me back until my ass is firmly planted over his raging boner.

Jesus, that thing's a fucking weapon ready to pop off the first chance it gets.

"*Ezra.* Seriously. You need to *rest.*"

He presses tender kisses to my shoulder blades, continuing his sleepy mumble. "I will rest better beside you. Do not leave." One of his palms dips between my thighs, and in a matter of moments, he's spreading me open and teasing my entrance with one of his thick fingers. He grunts apprecia-tively as I push back against him, slotting two knuckles inside me.

I bite my hand as he curls, slowly edging my pleasure higher. I hadn't planned for more sex so early in the morning, but now that we're here, I can't complain. My body temp rises and I'm grateful when Ezra drags the blankets off of me, leaving my body exposed to his intense gaze.

"Beautiful," he breathes, shifting suddenly so that he's sitting up on his knees. Grabbing my thigh, he holds it up at a ninety-degree angle against his torso. When the thick velvet length of his cock drags against my core, I moan at the blessed heat and the slick, wet sound as he glides easily by. He groans and repeats the motion torturously, brushing my clit in the slowest rhythm imaginable.

I've never been pulled open at such an intense angle, lying on my side as a man sinks deep with a simple thrust of his hips. He clasps his hands around my thigh to hold me in place. I reach for Ezra and touch the only part of him I can reach—his thigh—and feel the muscle contract as he moves.

I want to remind him that he's injured. That he shouldn't exert himself so much. That this isn't actually *resting*, and that it's not solving my overheating problem.

But all that comes out of my mouth is a series of stutters and broken words punctuated by deep moans as he touches the deepest parts of me and snares my pleasure within his own. He keeps the pace slow, and minutes pass in a beautiful crescendo of desire. I come before he does, clenching tightly around him and forgetting to breathe.

He chases his release with short, hard thrusts that fill the air with the slap of skin on skin and the liquid rush of desire dripping down our bodies. When he comes, I feel each burst as his cock twitches, an impossible warmth spilling inside me and leaking out onto the sheets. I'm too full of cum for it to be contained, although Ezra tries. He grinds his cock deep, getting as much of his seed as deep as he can.

As Ezra pulls out and even more cum follows his retreat, a shiver rolls down my spine. Where there should be post-coital bliss, instead, a flare of panic flickers in the back of my mind. Clarity hits a moment later, knocking the wind out of me.

I'm an *idiot*. What was it that Liam said, a week ago? That he wanted to be the one to knock me up before my men got the chance?

Icy dread wraps around the base of my spine, locking my body into place. *I'm not on protection.* Liam may no longer be a threat, thank god, but that doesn't mean we can afford to be reckless and keep having unprotected sex without thinking about the potential consequences. Very permanent, life-altering consequences. The kind that takes nine months to bake and a million hours to finally pop out of the oven once the timer goes off.

I told Andrei that I wasn't on birth control when we first had sex, but I never mentioned it to the others. Do they want me to get pregnant, or are we all fucking with reckless abandon because we can't control our impulses? Do we crave each other so much that we conveniently forget that actions like these have consequences?

I take shallow breaths as my panic increases. I could be pregnant right now. It's unlikely because I haven't ovulated yet, but you never know. Stranger things have happened, right? Didn't someone get pregnant from sitting on a toilet seat once? It doesn't take much to fertilize an egg, and I've had *three* men inside me within the past twenty-four hours. Their sperm must be fighting each other for the first shot at my next egg.

It's only a matter of time before it happens if we keep going like this.

Ezra notices the shift in my demeanor immediately, carefully lying back down beside me and lacing our fingers together. He brushes my knuckles with gentle sweeps of his thumb, flicking his eyes to mine. "What is on mind, Valentina?"

How do I tell the man who just came *so deep* inside me that I don't want kids?

I swallow thickly and sit up. Ezra's release follows gravity and seeps out onto the sheets. Normally, that would be hot as fuck. But while on the verge of a very untimely panic attack, it *sucks.* "I've gotta pee." I slip out of the bed and rush for the bathroom.

Before I make it halfway across the room, the bedroom door swings wide open and Mikhail bursts into the room with a plate of fried eggs. "Breakfast for the lazy couple—" He sees me first, his amber eyes sparkling above his signature Monrovia smile, until he senses that although I'm naked and thoroughly fucked, I'm not a shining beacon of warmth and happiness right now. Something's wrong. He knows it. Ezra knows it. It's only a matter of time before Andrei's husband senses start to tingle, and he rushes into the room to witness my breakdown.

I hate how well they can see through me.

"Be right back!"

As I lock the bathroom door, I can hear Mikhail hissing through his teeth. "*What did you do?*"

I automatically move to the shower and turn it on full blast. While the water heats, I clean up *down there* as much as I can and give myself a cursory glance in the mirror. Not only is my hair a rat's nest of knots and frizzed curls, but my body has remnants of bruises—whether hickeys or otherwise, I can't tell —but it looks like a war zone. Like a map of the past few weeks, seeping out of my body. I trace invisible lines from one bruise to the next, going through the events in my head as I touch each purple mark.

It's crazy, what I've been through lately.

Impossible, I would have said a year ago.

As steam fogs the mirror and blurs my reflection, I find myself laughing at the absurdity of everything.

I killed a man.

I step into the blistering hot shower and scrub my body from head to toe, trying to scourge the memory of Liam from my mind. The past week was filled with lies upon lies upon lies, from the words leaving my lips to the touches of my fingertips. Despite the heat, I shiver. I'm grateful to be back with my men, and I can already feel some of the stress ease from my muscles, but it's like one pain point disappears for another to take its place.

We haven't been using protection. I've known this in some capacity—it's impossible *not* to notice—but it hadn't really sunk in until Liam proudly declared that *he* would be the one to breed me.

My period arriving was a fucking *blessing*.

But I'm not sure a child would be. Not now, with a war brewing. And maybe not . . . ever. I grab a loofah and scrub beneath my fingernails, chipping away at dried flecks of blood and dirt. That's the problem, isn't it? The blood. *My* blood. Everyone's obsessed with the Baranova family—if I have a child, I'll just be bringing them into the same mess I was born into. The expectations and the power and the danger.

I don't want my child to be used as a bargaining chip for power. I don't want them to be abused because of their name and family line. And I can't guarantee that people won't come after them, like how Liam and Katya not only controlled my life for years but followed me once I'd left the city, just so that I would come back into the fold and play the part of perfect little princess.

When the water runs cold, I turn it off and stand shivering for as long as I can stand it. I'm not sure how Andrei will react when I tell him I don't want children. In the past, we were on the same page about having a family. I never had siblings, and Andrei never had a stable household. We'd intended to create an experience that neither of us had growing up. One full of love and laughter and warmth.

But after seeing the lengths people will go to claim the Bratva for themselves . . . I don't wish that upon anyone.

Maybe the Baranova line needs to end with me.

When I push open the shower door, I find Andrei leaning against the vanity, a small frown on his lips. I should have known that simple door locks are no match for these men. His eyes follow me as I grab a towel and wrap it around my body. I've never been able to tie a towel, so it's a surprise when it wraps neatly over my chest and I can tuck in the corner to hold it in place. I take another towel and wrap my hair.

Neither of us speaks until we're standing face to face, and there's nowhere for me to run.

"I don't think I want kids, Andrei."

If Andrei weren't breathing, I'd imagine he turned to stone. "We need an heir, *zhena*." He takes a deep breath, and I realize that he's wearing a plain white t-shirt and gray sweatpants. I've never seen him in either of those before. I've never imagined him in anything less than button ups and vests and expensive clothing. He looks more man than *pakhan*. Like flesh and blood and a desire for comfort at home, not like a ruthless leader ruling over a massive underground organization.

He looks like . . . *Andrei*.

I twist my fingers together as I try to detangle my thoughts. "I was given the Bratva by birth, but you, Andrei—you were chosen. You're not a Baranova. And you were chosen, anyway. You got the Bratva without me."

Andrei lifts a brow. "Someone had to marry you so that Tolkotsky could pass on the title. Bratvas are traditionally led by men. I was chosen, yes, but I was chosen to stand beside you."

I shake my head. "You don't understand. My father chose *you*, a man without a fortune, or a title, or a family name. You don't come from a well-known family. You don't have another Bratva waiting back home. You aren't trying to sow your seeds for political or social gain. And my father *still* chose you, because of how capable you had proven yourself. That has nothing to do with bloodline, and everything to do with ability." I close the short distance between us and cup Andrei's stubbled cheek in my palm. The dark circles under his eyes have lightened, but it will take much more R&R for them to disappear altogether. "Why can't we choose our successor without relying on my body to provide one? There's no guarantee I'd get pregnant, anyway, or that we wouldn't lose the baby—"

Andrei wraps his hand tight around mine, a sharpness to his gaze as he rises to his full height. "We wouldn't lose the baby, Valentina, despite how much you might wish to." His grip tightens, sending pain shooting into my wrist. But more painful than that are his words.

"I would *never* wish to lose—"

He cuts me off abruptly, venom dripping from his tone. "A child would be a blessing. They would be loved and cared for endlessly, because they won't have only two parents, but *four*. You realize that, don't you? It's not just you and me, Valentina, but it's Ezra and Mikhail too. You can't decide for all four of us if we're going to have kids or not. It needs to be a discussion, and one decided not because of what it means for the Bratva, but because of what it means for *us*." He releases my hand and narrows his gaze as he searches mine. "If you have objections to having children, we need to talk *now*. As

I'm sure you've realized, we're not keen on pulling out. You're at risk every time we so much as look in your direction, Valentina. We're ravenous for you *all the time*." His nostrils flare, and I can feel the hard point of his cock poking my stomach.

An angry boner, no doubt, but still a boner.

He screws his eyes shut on an exhale. "Mikhail made breakfast."

My stomach churns. "I'm not hungry."

"You need to eat." Turning the doorknob, Andrei pushes the door open to reveal both Mikhail and Ezra waiting—and listening—close by. "We need to talk. All four of us."

Ezra may still be naked, but his expression is unreadable as he stares at me. Mikhail, on the other hand, is red-faced and jumpy. The plate of eggs in his hand bounces up and down as he taps his foot, a vein in his neck throbbing as he swallows whatever is on his mind.

Being with them again after a week apart has been a soothing balm on all our wounds. If anything is going to disturb the peace, I guess I'm grateful that it's only me this time, and not a threat from the outside.

Just me, and the one thing that could tear us all apart.

The truth.

CHAPTER 15

EZRA

ANY TIME I've been around babies, their tiny eyes have watered and their little voices have wailed. Whether it's my blank stare that sets them off, or the fresh bruises on my knuckles, or the way their mothers clutch them tighter to their chests as I walk past, I can't say.

I just know that after one look at me, they cry.

I've seen people coo at babies or sing to them to put an end to their tears. Sometimes, I get the urge to try. Maybe I can make a baby laugh, and their parent won't curl their lip as they walk away from me. Maybe, one laughing baby at a time, things will change. But by the time I remember to smile, the family has moved on. I'm standing alone on the sidewalk.

The only way I might spend time with a baby, then, is if I either steal one—which won't win me any points with my future wife—or if I have my own.

Creating a child is laughably easy for most men. It's unplanned, or it's instinctual, or it could actually be a beautiful moment that's been planned and prayed for night after night upon every wishing star in the sky.

But for many of us, that simply isn't the case. Andrei's

father is nameless. Mikhail's stuck around until things got tough. My own father decided to have as many sons as possible so that he could strengthen the numbers of the Russian Bratva by merit of his cock, instead of his fists. Thankfully, he only had one child—a son he had no interest in raising. He tossed me into the Bratva and let the *vors* raise me with harsh words and even harsher fists, but even then, I can't say that the Bratva ever treated me like a proper son.

I was a dog to train for the fighting pits.

The most experience I have with flesh and blood fathers doing their actual jobs is from watching the ones within the Baranova Bratva raise their sons and spoil their daughters. It's not often that I see the children in our sector—my line of work lends itself more to brawls and blood than toys and toddlers—but when I catch a glimpse of parenthood, I get a sense that the job is difficult sometimes, but no less important.

Maybe even *rewarding*.

As Valentina plays with the cold eggs and limp toast on her plate, I wonder how she would look with a baby—*my* baby— in her arms. Raven-colored hair, like mine. Curled, like hers. Tiny dimples when she smiles. A laugh that lights up the room.

I've never pictured myself as a father. I've never *wanted* to be a father. How could I, after the failings of my own? Of Andrei's and Mikhail's? But Valentina brings a layer of peace and comfort to our lives that makes me wonder if I *could* step away from the blood and bone, and give parenthood a try.

I quickly scan Valentina's body for signs of pregnancy. I don't actually know much about how it works, other than the basics. Is it too soon to know? Would she be able to feel a change in her body, or would we need a test to find out? A dozen questions zip through my mind too fast for me to latch onto, but the most important ones ring clear as a bell.

Could I be a father?

Would I be any good at it?

Once Valentina threw on one of Mikhail's t-shirts and boxers after her shower, she joined the three of us in the kitchen. Mikhail's beach house is his personal retreat—no one is allowed inside without his express permission. I've only been here twice before. Judging by the lack of women's clothing and toiletries I've failed to locate on both of my previous surveys of the house, I suspect that he's never brought a woman here before, which makes Valentina the first. She may not realize how privileged a position that is.

I doubt he'll ever tell her.

Valentina flicks her eyes between each of us and sits at the place Mikhail set out for her at the breakfast table. Two fried eggs and toast, with a glass of orange juice. A true bachelor's breakfast. She eyes the food warily. "I don't know what more you want me to say. You heard everything."

Andrei leans closer, resting his elbows along the table's edge. "Say it again, so that we *all* hear it. Directly. From. You."

Mikhail hovers behind us, a scowl etched across his features. If anyone should be kneeling at Valentina's feet to give her anything and everything she wants, it should be *Mr. Obsessed* himself. So, she doesn't want kids? Ply her with jewels and expensive dinners and trips to Venice. He's never expressed wanting to have kids before; falling for Valentina shouldn't be a big deal. It shouldn't change his mind about how he wants to live his life—or with whom.

My chest tightens as my eyes lock with hers. One woman *shouldn't* change any of our stances on having children. We're men of the Russian Bratva—we live violent lives. There is no place for something as innocent as a child in our line of work —or our personal lives. We'll fuck things up, for sure, without even trying. Hell, even Tolkotsky's relationship with Valentina was strained at best. After our own father figures failed us, none of us should *want* children.

But despite all of the shit from our individual pasts, Valentina somehow makes us want . . . more than we've imagined. More than we ever thought possible. A child? A *family*? A living, breathing, happy group of people coexisting under one roof. It's not just me and Valentina raising a child together —it's *all* of us. And that makes the challenge feel a hell of a lot less impossible and more . . . *real*.

Valentina gives me hope for the future in a way that I've never felt before.

Valentina clasps her hands in her lap, straightens her spine, and looks me in my eyes for what comes next. My world suddenly shrinks back down from the potential *all of us* to only *us* in an instant. I can feel the way she's tuned into the frequency in my bones. *Locked in* with me, willingly. The man she should have never wanted, yet chose anyway.

I'm eternally grateful for that decision.

My pulse hammers through my veins all the same, nearly drowning out her voice.

"I don't think I want to have kids."

I don't get a chance to respond.

"You don't *think* you want to have kids? That's something you really should *know*, Valentina. Way before having unprotected sex with all three of us." Andrei is clearly hot about the subject, absentmindedly tapping his heel against the tile floor. "You could be pregnant right now."

Valentina rolls her eyes. "I just had my period."

Andrei's eyes narrow. "We came inside you last night, and I'm sure Ezra did again this morning."

Valentina's cheeks flush, and despite the ripple of agitation manifesting across her face, she's damn beautiful. Sunlight streams through the oceanfront windows, casting warm, orange streaks across her hair and shoulders. "Could you stop with the melodramatic shit, Andrei? Yes, we've all had sex. It's been one big fucking orgy after another. But that doesn't change the fact that I don't want kids!"

Mikhail's voice is calmer than Andrei's, for once. "What's changed?"

"Everything, obviously!" Valentina scrubs a hand down her face and rubs the back of her eyelids. "Liam kidnapped me, you guys. *Me.* The Baranova Princess, in a chapel full of witnesses, in broad fucking daylight. If he can get to me that easily, who's to say that someone else can't get to our children? Steal them out from under our noses, in our own home?" Shaking her head, she sighs. "I don't want them to go through anything like that. Grant me at least one shred of grace and understand that I *know* what we're giving up. Having a child would be—" her voice cracks, sharpening her next inhale— "they deserve better than what we can give them."

My shoulder aches as Valentina stares at it, digging beneath the bandages and gauze to picture the wound and its inevitable scarring. I shift my arm in its sling, careful to keep the discomfort off my face.

Mikhail opens his mouth, but I cut him off before he can jump down Valentina's throat and make things worse. "You are right, child deserves best life." Stretching out my legs, I nudge Valentina's foot with mine. The flicker of surprise across her face releases some of the tension in her shoulders. I continue, "but best life is with loving family. *We* are loving family. Bloodied and bruised, yes, but loving. We protect our own. We will protect child with last breath." I incline my head towards our woman, hoping she understands that even though her fears are valid, so too are our reasons. "Like we will protect wife and mother, and each other. With last breath."

Mikhail grabs the back of my chair as an anchor and wedges himself in the infinitesimal gap between Andrei and my shoulders. "You were kidnapped because we were arrogant and careless. No one's ever challenged us like that before, especially not in our territory. Most people know not to fuck with the *pakhan*, but our reign is new and, before now, untested." He gestures vaguely towards Valentina. "We don't have decades of family lineage backing our claim." With a sigh, he runs a hand through his hair, destroying what semblance of *normal* he has left. His hair sticks out on all sides, and the five o'clock shadow working its way across his jaw is *begging* to be shaved. "What happened to you was a mistake, one that we'll pay for for the rest of our lives."

"That we will *atone* for," Andrei revises.

"That's what I said," Mikhail grumbles, glaring at the back of Andrei's head.

I nudge Valentina's knee to regain her attention. She needs reassurance, and I will give it to her every fucking day of the year if I have to. Whatever it takes to let her know that not only are we sorry for fucking up, but it will *never* happen again. "*Lisichka.* I make promise." Snagging her hand under the table, I lace our fingers together and squeeze. "I will kill every man and woman who threatens family. Idle threat. Real threat. Does not matter. They will not breathe next breath, because I will crush lungs with bare hands. I will bring fear of God, and they will remember it, or they will die."

"She doesn't need a death poem, for fuck's sake." I can't see Mikhail over my shoulder, but I can hear the eye roll. "Once we prove to everyone that we're dangerous fuckers, no one will try this shit again, is what Ezra's trying to say." He pinches the bridge of his nose before taking a quick breath. "Baby, I know you can't trust us so soon after this bullshit with Liam and Katya, but I swear, it won't happen again. Not to you, or to any future kids of ours. But, love, we won't be the only ones looking out for our family. We have an entire Bratva behind us. *They* are family, too. They'll keep us safe, just like we'll keep them safe."

Valentina purses her lips. "Because that worked so well before."

Mikhail's expression hardens. "It's different now. Katya isn't around to fuck with things. We have you, and it's going to stay that way. The Bratva will see your devotion to us, and the *mudaks* who doubted it will realize how fucking stupid they've been. They'll come crawling back on their hands and knees, begging for forgiveness."

"They are all dead." I shrug with my good shoulder. "No one left to beg."

Valentina's eyes widen. "What do you mean by that, Ezra?"

My phone buzzes in my pocket, but I don't need to check it to know what the messages say. We gave the final kill order last night. Anyone whose loyalty has wavered over the past few weeks should be dead by now. There is no room for the weak in our ranks. "They are dead," I repeat. "All seventy-five."

Andrei keeps detailed records of every single member of the Bratva. After Valentina's abduction, we checked every single one. Those who abandoned us for Katya were marked immediately. A few upstarts never made it out of the chapel. Their blood stains the floors.

With a shrug, Mikhail continues. "The others won't be foolish enough to follow them, then. Especially once they see that Valentina remains by our side."

"You killed seventy-five people?" Valentina swallows thickly.

I nod. "No one will hurt you again, *lisichka*. I promise."

"*We* promise." Mikhail reaches across the table and cups Valentina's face in his hands. "So don't shut out the idea of kids just yet, okay?" As he leans across the table to reach her, he knocks her glass to the floor and shuts both me and Andrei out completely. The words he whispers against her lips betray a gentleness that his touch foregoes. "We deserve our own happiness, don't you think?"

Tears fill Valentina's eyes, and if it weren't for fucking Mikhail, I'd kiss them all away. The bastard gets to them first, sucking each one against his lips the moment they slide down her cheeks. When he kisses her on the lips, she melts in her chair. I'm both relieved that she's relaxing *and* annoyed that it's not with me. I nudge Mikhail's hip hard, knocking him off balance. He snaps back with *anger* in his eyes, like I interrupted his favorite meal.

Too fucking bad.

Andrei steals the advantage and rounds the table to Valentina's side. He kneels at her feet and kisses both of her hands. "A queen deserves a loyal kingdom. The Bratva will fight to protect our family just as strongly as they'll fight to protect their own. You'll see."

"We must give them something fight for." I nod towards Andrei. "We will give them marriage."

"And babies," Mikhail adds, "lots of babies."

"I haven't said yes yet," Valentina reminds us. "I . . . need some time to think. About kids, not about marriage."

Andrei kisses each of Valentina's palms. "Take all the time you need, love."

She exhales slowly, then nods. "Okay. Thank you."

My phone buzzes again. Andrei and I share a look. I bet his is going off more than mine. I only have to deal with our Bratva, but Andrei has to deal with the world. After Valentina's disappearance—and now the Mayor's, I'm sure—high-ranking officials within the city have questions. It's easy enough to smooth things over, but it *does* take an appearance or two to do it.

But the last thing I want to do is deal with Bratva duties today. Valentina's hand is warm in mine, and I sweep my thumb across her knuckles. We could have lost her. This whole thing we have going for us could have come crumbling down in an instant. We wouldn't be talking about babies, we'd be best friends with the bottom of a bottle.

Speaking of which, I spot a high-dollar vodka calling my name. I slip away to snag the bottle and pour two new glasses of orange juice, one with a heavy dose of Russian medicine. While someone cleans up the spill on the hardwood, I hand Valentina the fresh glass and sit across from her.

She relaxes further as she takes a tiny sip. "What do we do now?"

"We eat." I jab Valentina's fork into a blob of egg whites and hold it up to her lips. It looks disgusting. It *wobbles*. "We rest."

"We fuck, like rabbits." Mikhail drags his chair next to Valentina and places his hands on her thighs, spreading them just enough to tease her inner thighs.

Valentina flushes pink, but she doesn't stop him. He buries his face in her hair and sighs as he lovingly squeezes her thighs, grabs her hips, rubs her stomach. "You felt so fucking perfect, squeezing my cock last night, *malyshka*. I'm an addict for your pussy. And this perfect body—" He groans in the back of his throat as his hands wander the expanse of her body, squeezing her breasts, palming her curves, lifting her shirt to kiss her stomach. "Breathtaking." He dives to his knees in front of her and shoulders her thighs apart even more, making room for himself. "I need a taste."

She squeaks when he pulls her ass to the edge of her seat. "M-Mikhail," Valentina whispers, fisting his hair. "We shouldn't—" Her eyes screw shut the moment he buries his face deeper and latches onto her sex through the boxers she's wearing.

I lean back in my chair to block Mikhail from view beneath the table. Taking a swig of my drink, I study Valentina's blushing face. Her eyes are closed, her mouth open in a pretty *O*. "Open your eyes, *lisichka*. Let us see how good you feel."

She shakes her head. "N-no. We shouldn't—"

The sound of fabric tearing fills the air as Mikhail shreds the thin barrier between them. He groans, and Valentina's back arches a second later.

Andrei stands beside Valentina and grabs her chin, wrenching her face towards him. "Why not, *zhena*? We want to please you."

With one hand keeping Mikhail firmly in place, she grabs Andrei's arm with the other. "Normal breakfast—we should have a—*ahh*—normal morning together."

I down the rest of my juice and pour straight vodka next. My cock fills as Valentina tries to maintain her composure. I wish she would open her eyes. I want to watch them blow wide open when she comes. "This is normal, no? You have breakfast, we have breakfast." I spot Andrei adjusting himself, his cock already at full mast.

I came once this morning. I'm allowed to take a little longer to get there. I put my feet up on an empty chair and pull my cock free, stroking it to each breathless sound Valentina makes.

"Perfectly normal," Andrei agrees, cupping Valentina's face. He leans down and takes her mouth in his, slipping his tongue between her lips. They both moan, and Valentina moves her hand from his arm to the thick bulge between them. She rubs him eagerly as he rocks his hips into her palm.

Our girl is just as horny as us. This will definitely be our new normal, from now on.

"Bring her here." I pat the table in front of me. "I am hungry."

Mikhail lifts his hand above the table to flick me off.

But Valentina finally opens her eyes and looks at me. A little dazed, a lot horny, face flushed and lips swollen. She pushes Mikhail and Andrei back to stand up. But before she can walk over to my side of the table, Mikhail quickly sweeps everything on it to the floor and Andrei lifts her, lying her flat on her stomach, facing me. The table is short enough that her ass dangles off one end, with her face perfectly level with mine at the other.

"Hello, beautiful." I drop my empty glass to the floor and brush a handful of curls behind her ear. "Can we fuck you?" I doubt Mikhail would bother asking, but after she ran from me this morning, I want to know that she trusts us. That she wants us. That she is okay with fucking us raw—even if it means she could get pregnant. "Can we fill up perfect pussy?"

Her eyes glaze over, and I glance up to catch Andrei working her with his fingers. She's so wet that we can *hear* it.

I'm not sure that she heard my question. I shake my head at Andrei, and thankfully he pulls his fingers free. I catch him pumping his dick with his wet fingers. At some point, Mikhail stripped naked, baring all for the room.

The horny fucker.

Taking Valentina's face gently in my hands, I brush my thumbs across her cheeks. "Does our queen want her king?"

Valentina bites her bottom lip and meets my eyes. My heart skips a beat as she wraps her arms around my neck and sighs against my lips. "I want all three of my kings, Ezra. You'll fuck me too, won't you? You'll fill me up, and put a baby in me—"

The air rushes from my lungs as the world collapses once more to just me and her. *A baby*. With me. An adorable little girl, or a shy little boy, or an adventurous troublemaker. *Ours*. My cock swells to the point of pain, and my balls tighten prematurely. "Are you sure?"

I don't know if I'll be any good at parenting. I might be too firm, or too soft, or too quiet, or too busy. I might feed them too much sugar, or bounce them too hard on my knee, or give them their first taste of vodka too young for her liking. I might fuck it all up.

Or. It might be better than I can imagine. Because it will be with the love of my life.

Valentina takes a breath. "Mikhail will spoil them rotten, and Andrei will proudly show them to the world." She touches my chest. "But you, Ezra, will love and protect them fiercer than anyone. How could I not want them to have a father like that? How could I not want *you*?" She kisses me sweetly, but I kiss her *hard*.

All of my doubts melt away until there's nothing left but *love*. I won't be a perfect father, but she believes in me. And that's enough. She moans into my mouth and grabs onto my shoulders, adjusting her position on the table so that her knees are spread wide and her ass hangs low, baring herself to the others.

When Andrei surges inside her, our kiss deepens. I'm lost in this woman, my heart gripped firmly in her fists. She claws at my shoulders as Andrei thrusts hard and deep, the smack of his hips against her ass filling the room. My cock jerks as precum dribbles from the tip, and I grip it hard to keep it from spilling.

Every last drop needs to be for her.

"Hurry up," Mikhail whines, "I'm aching to knock her up first."

"Wait your turn." Andrei grinds deep, growling in the back of his throat. "The first baby is mine. We need a strong heir."

Valentina pushes back onto his cock, meeting each of his thrusts.

"*Fuck*, that's gonna make me—" He groans and buries himself deep. Valentina whimpers into my ear, and it's one of the best fucking things I've ever heard.

"That is one," I murmur, "how many more can you take, hm? Two? Three?"

Once Andrei moves out of his way, Mikhail plays with her pussy lips, rubbing the head of his cock through her folds. "It's dripping out. We can't have that, now, can we?" He sinks inside with a hiss, tossing his head back. "Such a wet fucking mess. *God*, you feel so fucking—" He curses in Russian and pounds inside her fast, digging his nails into the globes of her ass.

Valentina yelps, but I lick into her mouth and steal the sound. I cup her breasts beneath her shirt and massage them hard, making her moan, helping her relax. She needs to come if we're going to fuck her brains out.

I play with her nipples, rubbing circles around them, pinching them between my fingertips. Lowering my head, I wrap my lips around one and suck, earning a low moan from our queen.

Someone spits, and Valentina's breath catches.

"Relax, *zhena*, I want to make you feel good. Let me in."

Ah, Andrei is playing with her ass.

She whines, and I double my efforts to make her come. "So full, *lisichka*. Naughty little fox, demanding three men. Can you handle another cock? I have load ready for you."

Fuck, I'm so hard that it hurts. If she says no, I'll grit my teeth and bare it, but if she says *yes*—

Her voice is strong when she replies, and thank the gods it's a *yes*.

I pull off her breasts and stand in front of her face. She opens her mouth in a lewd display of desire, staring at my erection. I hold it in my fist and pump it nice and slow for her to see. "I only give cock to good girl. Are you good girl, Valentina?"

"*Yes.*"

I wrap my fingers in her hair but hold her back. Her warm

breath surrounds my length, making it twitch harder. "Mikhail, rub her clit." When Valentina's body jerks, I know he's made contact. I rub the tip of my cock against Valentina's lips, smearing her with my scent. She flicks her tongue against my weeping slit, and my balls fucking *hurt*. They're swollen, too. *Fuck*, this is going to be a big load.

"You will come with me, yes?"

Valentina nods enthusiastically, and I push the head of my dick past her lips. She closes her eyes with a moan, and I have to fight not to come then and there. I help her swallow me down, pushing on the back of her head when she stalls. Her nostrils flare, and tears fill her eyes. But she doesn't pull back —she hollows out her cheeks and *sucks*.

Holy fucking shiiiiiit—

A growl catches in my throat as I start fucking her face, unable to be gentle when she opens her eyes and *looks at me*. Saliva drips down her chin, tears slide down her cheeks, but somehow, her emerald eyes shine brighter than ever as we claim her pussy, ass, and mouth. All three of us, working in tandem.

All four of us about to come *hard*.

"*Now*," I snarl, forcing my cock to the back of her throat as I explode, my muscles tightening, my body rushing with endorphins. I can't stop it. I pump her mouth full of me, one pulse at a time, as Andrei growls and slams *hard* into her, filling up hole number two.

Mikhail comes across her back, pumping most of his release against the tight ring of her asshole and between her cheeks. He must have fingered her ass, otherwise she'd be pumped full in hole number three, too. He uses his finger to push some of it inside and play with her some more, stretching her out, getting her used to the feel of it. She clenches around his finger and her body convulses a second time.

Fuck me, did she just come from that?

She taps my thigh and I quickly pull out. I hadn't meant to stay back there so long. I hold her face as she gasps for air.

Cum drips down her chin, and I know her pussy's leaking, too. Mikhail did a good enough job of coming on her ass because even though he didn't fuck her there, it *looks* like he did.

Valentina's a fucking mess, and she's *smiling* about it. "Filled me up so good," she murmurs, shutting her eyes. "S'good."

I kiss the top of her head. "Good girls get filled."

"Good girls *also* get naps." She melts on the table, and Mikhail and Andrei work together to carry her back to the bedroom.

As they leave, I pat my pockets for a cigarette. Once it's lit between my fingers, I stare at the smoke curling in the air.

For once, I don't crave the hit.

I set it down on the table and watch the end burn out, feeling a sense of finality wash over me. If I'm going to be a father, I better live long enough to see it.

CHAPTER 16

ANDREI

MY WIFE IS SMILING. It's the tiniest curve of her lips, a simple hint of her feelings, and yet it fills me with as much joy as when I'm buried deep inside her. All-encompassing, warm *happiness.*

During the years after Valentina left, I resigned myself to a life without. I was destined for a life of brutality without the solace of home—a place of rest after long days and nights maintaining order and safeguarding our Bratva.

Valentina returning home and choosing to stay with me—with us—has been an antidote to the bitter poison pumping through my veins. I can have everything I've ever wanted, all thanks to my queen.

It's a debt I will repay for the rest of my life.

Her idle smile grows as she watches Mikhail and Ezra sign their names on their own marriage certificates. She will be recognized as my wife within state and federal bounds, but she will be considered all three of our wives, for all intents and purposes. More importantly, the Bratva will recognize our polyamorous union.

I nod to our lawyer, who signs as witness on all documents

before carefully clasping them within his briefcase. Valentina thanks him, and then Mikhail walks him outside to rejoin his guarded escort back within city limits.

Taking Valentina's hand in mine, I lift her ring to my lips. "You deserve more than this." We had a perfect wedding planned, *twice*. Scores of people gathered in celebration, more gifts than could be counted, a magnificent venue draped in silks and adorned with two florists' worth of bouquets. *That* is what Valentina deserves—*everything*. Not a boring legal procedure. Not a white T-shirt and silk shorts. No jewels, roses, or pretty things in sight.

Just a beach house, and her three sex-crazed men.

Valentina meets my eyes. "This is perfect, Andrei. I don't need a spectacle. I only need you." She steps into my arms and presses a gentle kiss to my jaw. "I'm happy to do it this way, without all the fuss."

I brush my fingertips across the expanse of her neck, imagining Liam's drug-laced needle. The way he must have dragged her from the chapel. Ripped off her veil. Terrified her.

It's no wonder she doesn't want a large ceremony. She may never want to attend a wedding again. I can't say that I blame her. Some might call two botched weddings a bad omen, and a third attempt would be an affront to the gods. I don't care about the gods or their designs. I care about my wife and her well-being.

If she doesn't want a wedding, so be it.

I press a kiss to her forehead. "How are you feeling?" We haven't discussed Liam's death, or Katya's, for that matter. It feels like we've barely had room to breathe, and in that space, all we've done is fuck.

Not that I regret the sex. But it's easy to mask trauma beneath layers of desire.

She hesitates before answering. "I'm glad to be married, but I can't say that I know what comes next." We've spent the past two days recovering and ignoring the outside world. When Valentina sleeps, or showers, or gets pounded by my brothers, sometimes I slip away to check the state of things.

Sadly, it's not as stable as it should be. After Liam's death, as predicted, another usurper emerged from the chaos. Thankfully, this one has no backing. But it's another life to take, and although I have no qualms about snuffing out weakness, Valentina deserves to be in the know for these decisions from now on.

I've been waiting for the right moment to tell her. Our little escape doesn't exactly scream honeymoon, but I hate to ruin the peace after a week of pure shit. We deserve an entire month of drowning in each other.

I'll make sure we get it.

"We've been resting and fucking, as planned." I wrap my arms around Valentina's waist, laying my hands on her ass. I don't like seeing her in Mikhail's clothes, so she needs to be naked. Immediately.

I continue speaking as I pull down her shorts. "But we need to get back. There's unfinished business with the Russian transfers, and we need to decide what to do with Francesca and the orphanage. Then there's Anton Dolohov, who survived the ambush at the mayor's mansion."

She pulls off her shirt and steps out of her bottoms for me. "Is this really what you want to be talking about right now?" She grabs her tits and pushes them together, raising an eyebrow at me. "Or do you want to fuck your wife?"

My cock pulses. I love when she's bold. "You want me to fuck you, *zhena*? Have you been neglected for too long?"

She nods, hunger flashing in her eyes. "I want my husband to fuck me, yes."

As I pull off my shirt, Mikhail slips between us and drops to his knees, already lifting Valentina's knee to prop it over his shoulder. "Which one?" He kisses her inner thighs, inching his way higher with each press of his lips. "You have three now."

Ezra moves behind Valentina and pulls her against his chest, holding her steady while Mikhail works his tongue against her. Her breath catches. "A-all of them," she sighs, leaning into Ezra's embrace. He sucks on her neck, and her eyes flutter closed. "I want all of you inside me."

I chuckle. "I doubt all three of us can fit at the same time, darling."

"We can try."

I freeze, my hand hovering on my waistband. She can't mean that. Can she? I lock eyes with Ezra. He's just as intrigued as I am. Mikhail doubles his efforts, spreading Valentina's lips to suck on her clit and slip two fingers inside her heat. He groans against her pussy, liking the idea, too.

"What better way to christen marriage," Ezra rumbles, his dark eyes pitching to black, "than taking wife together."

Valentina's legs start to tremble, her breaths puffing in short, little pants. "P-please. I want it. Please fill me with your cocks. All of them." Her body seizes as she comes from either the idea or Mikhail's skilled work. Ezra claims her mouth greedily, sucking her bottom lip between his.

I've always been a jealous, possessive man, but seeing Valentina ravaged by my best men is another kind of high. My cock aches to be inside her. I quickly undress and scoop Valentina into my arms. We make it to the master suite in record time. Gently setting her down on the bed, I climb on top of her, kissing her with all of my strength. She holds onto my shoulders as I drag her higher up onto the mattress. "If this is going to work, you'll need to be on top."

Ezra, Mikhail, and I have already discussed logistics. There are a few different poses we'd like to try, but for our first time, we want Valentina on full display. She can control the pace at first if she wants, until she adjusts. But once we're all inside of her, I don't know that we'll be able to hold back.

She'll have to take it from all three of us, all at once.

I kiss Valentina one last time before letting Ezra take over. He slides onto the mattress and flips Valentina with one arm, still way too damned strong despite his injuries. But fuck, I love seeing Valentina overpowered. Her hair flares out around her face as she settles over Ezra's hips. She bites her lip and brushes her curls over one shoulder. "How are we going to do this?"

Ezra runs his palms up and down her thighs. "Do not think. Feel."

While Valentina rubs her slick heat over Ezra's cock, Mikhail lubes up his fingers, then kneels behind her. He kisses her shoulders, then rasps in her ear. "I'm gonna to take you from behind, baby. Right here."

Valentina's eyes flutter closed. "O-*oh*. Will it fit?"

He hums an *mhm* as he sucks a bruise on the side of her neck. "I promise, it'll fucking fit. You're gonna be so stuffed full of cock; it's gonna be so *fucking* hot. Now, sit on Ezra's dick, love, that's it. *That's it.*"

Valentina slowly slides on top of Ezra, one agonizing inch at a time. His entire body freezes to give her time to adjust, but Mikhail isn't as patient. He slips a finger into her ass and plays with her back entrance, keeping a hand on her hip to ensure she keeps rocking back and forth on Ezra's cock and his finger.

I should demand him to take it slow, but one look at Valentina's face screams *no fucking way*. Her face flushes crimson, her lips parted *just enough*, and she's looking directly at me.

"You're beautiful, *zhena*, so fucking beautiful riding Ezra's cock. Do you know how gorgeous you are?"

She shakes her head.

My mouth waters as her tits bounce. But beyond her body

is the woman who accepts all three of us, who *loves* all three of us, and invites us into her bed and her heart, all at once.

A woman who can love three wicked hearts like ours is a fucking angel.

"You capture my heart and soul with a single glance, *zhena*. Men would go to war for a glimpse of your beauty, baby." My eyes wander her body, taking in her thick thighs, her round belly, her voluptuous tits, her deep emerald eyes, the freckles painting her skin. She is *perfect*. A fucking goddess. "But I'll kill any man who so much as stares, Valentina. Who dares imagine what's mine. Your body is *mine*. Your heart is *mine*. Your life is fucking *mine*."

"*Ours*," Mikhail corrects, grumbling the word against her skin.

God, my cock fucking *hurts*. It throbs painfully, larger than usual, and I need to be inside my wife right fucking now. I grab the bottle of lube and apply a generous amount to my swollen member.

I'm gonna fuck my wife, no matter what. I can't wait any longer.

I kneel over Ezra's chest and lean Valentina back to make room for me. I grip my cock hard and smack it against her clit. She bucks, gasping. "W-what are you doing?"

Ezra grunts beneath us, probably disliking my change of plans, but too fucking bad.

I need her.

"Hover over the tip, *zhena*, good. Hold it, just like that." It's going to be a tight fit, but it will work. I know it will. I press my cock against Ezra's and notch myself at the front of Valentina's pussy. Mikhail pushes down on Valentina's shoulders as the three of us work together to impale Valentina on *two* cocks.

Ezra grits his teeth. "*Mikhail*. Remove fingers."

Mikhail laughs. "Fuck no. She's clenched so fucking tight.

You like my fingers in your ass, don't you, *malyshka*?" He nibbles on her earlobe, groaning when she finally nods. "See? She can take it."

A vein in her neck pulses.

I wrap my palm around her throat. She's not breathing. "Breathe, love. That's an order."

Once she fills her lungs, I squeeze just enough to cut off some of her circulation. Her eyes bulge, but when I thrust another inch inside her pussy, she moans *loud*. All four of us shudder as she slips down another inch.

Fuck me. It's tight. I can feel Ezra's heartbeat in his cock. Or is that mine? Valentina's desire drips down our lengths, but the lube definitely helps. "You will breathe every time we pull back, understand?"

She nods, and I tighten my grip as I plunge deeper.

Holy fucking shit.

Not only is she gripping me like a vice, but Ezra's dick rubs against mine, an extra layer of heat and friction as we both struggle to fuck Valentina harder. Eventually, we find a rhythm, the two of us grunting and groaning every time Valentina twitches. She does as she's told and breathes every time we pull out, and her obedience is enough to bring me to the edge.

I smash our lips together with a growl, pumping my hips harder, hearing her squeal but not caring, too far gone to stop.

I come first, as deep as possible with Ezra in the fucking way, and then Ezra groans and follows immediately. Our cum drips onto the sheets, but I'm not ready to pull out completely.

Mikhail thrusts hard from behind Valentina, and she gasps in a breath. I release her throat, but she latches onto my shoulders, digging her nails into my skin as she holds onto me for dear life. "*Ohhhh*. Fuck. Fuckfuckfuck."

Reaching between us, I rub my cum over her clit in tight

circles, enjoying the way her body twitches. "Is Mikhail inside you, baby?" The wet smack of his hips against her ass is proof enough, but I want to hear her say it. "Is he fucking you in the ass?"

"Yes," she cries, burying her face in my neck.

Ezra thrusts his hips up, grunting as he fills her pussy again.

Fuck, can we go another round?

I replace my fingers with my cock and rub against Valentina's clit, my eyes rolling back at how fucking wet it is down there. She convulses in my arms, and I lock my arms around her ribs to keep her in place. "Does he feel good?" I groan in her ear. "He's going to come in your ass, Valentina. You're such a dirty wife, taking three cocks and multiple loads. I bet you want more cum, don't you?" I can't tell if she's listening; her eyes are screwed shut and she's forgetting to breathe again.

Mikhail bites her shoulder and growls. "Fucking come, Valentina! Come on my cock buried in your tight little ass!" He slams hard, and she *screams* as she comes. Ezra and Mikhail freeze as she tightens around them, but I'm free to continue stroking her clit. I work her through her orgasm, grunting in her ear as my own pleasure builds.

I'm going to come again. *Fuck*, I'm going to come again. *Fuckfuckfuck*—

My balls tighten, and I come just as hard as the first time. My dick pulses as I paint her clit white. Ezra curses in Russian and groans, likely filling her up deeper this time.

Mikhail fucking *roars*.

We all pull out and collapse in a heap of limbs, making sure Valentina is wedged in the middle with her head on the pillow. I'm not sure whose arm is over mine or whose dick is on my thigh, but I don't fucking care.

I'd give my life for these men. If they work just as hard at pleasuring and protecting Valentina as I do, I have no complaints.

Even with two extra limp dicks in the bed.

None of us want to move, but it's Valentina's mumbled *water* that gets me out of bed. I chug one glass of water and bring three more back to the bedroom, but by the time I've returned, Ezra is passed out and Valentina is mumbling something into Mikhail's chest. He sweeps his hand across her back, whispering something back to her that I can't hear.

I should be jealous of their intimacy, but I feel lighter than I have in years.

Valentina is still smiling.

That makes everything worth it.

CHAPTER 17

VALENTINA

A MOAN SLIPS past my lips as Mikhail's fingers dig into my scalp, scrubbing soap into my hair. I dip my chin lower as my eyes flutter closed. *This* is the life—soaking in a huge, clawfoot tub, with one of the men I love nestled against my back.

He kisses the nape of my neck with a pleased hum. "I think, as long as you're here with me, love, this is my new favorite feature of the house." One of his hands slips beneath the steaming water to cup my breast. "I've never enjoyed a bath as much as this."

Ezra grumbles from across the bathroom, his eyebrows pinched together as he watches Mikhail fondle me in the tub. "You would think with million dollars, he would buy bigger tub," he mutters, pinching an unlit cigarette between his teeth. It's become his latest habit—hold the smoke, but don't light it. Chew on the end, perhaps, or tap the pack against his thigh, but I haven't seen him light a cigarette since the night he admitted he wasn't sleeping.

Whatever his reason, I'm grateful for it.

"You should *really* consider an upgrade," I agree, sighing

as Mikhail stops teasing me to knead my shoulders. "Then we'd all fit instead of just you and me."

"I *like* it being just the two of us, *malyshka*. Imagine how dirty the water would get with those two in here." He clicks his tongue and digs harder into my muscles. "You know what, *don't* imagine it. I want you all to myself, even your thoughts." He lifts his eyes to glare at Ezra. "*Someone* should really catch the hint and leave us alone. Newlyweds need their alone time."

Ezra scoffs. "She is not only your wife."

Mikhail scrubs the conditioner from my hair. "She is when she's with me," he sighs, dipping his hands beneath the water to stroke my bare skin. "Naked and wanting —*trembling*, even. Isn't that right, love?" He kisses behind my ear, stroking my stomach with one hand while the other slips between my thighs. I bend my knees to grant him access, and he immediately pinpoints my clit with his deft fingers. Each stroke is slow and sensuous, stoking the fires of my desire.

I lay my head against his shoulder and relax against him. "It's a dirty trick to keep—*ahh*!" Jolts of pleasure radiate deep inside as Mikhail picks up the pace. "K-keep me—the tub isn't even—*Mikhail*," I whine. "S-stop, wait—"

"*No.*" He lifts my leg onto the edge of the tub, spreading me open. "You're mine for the hour, Valentina, and I intend to enjoy every second of it." His fingers slide lower, sinking into my core with ease. As he pumps them inside me, he digs the heel of his palm against my clit. It *hurts*, I'm so sensitive, but it also feels—

"*So good*," Mikhail rasps, groaning as I start to tremble. "You're gonna come for me, baby. Squeeze my fingers."

I squeeze my walls as tight as I can, and he rewards me with a growl. "*Fuck*, that's hot. So fucking tight. You like me inside you, don't you, Valentina? Say it." Water sloshes over the edge of the tub, splashing on the tiles. But Mikhail doesn't stop; he goes *harder*, curling a third finger inside and hitting something *deep*.

Gasping, I clutch the edges of the tub as white-hot pleasure zips through me. I'm close—*so close*—but my body's so hot that I don't think I can make it. I'm going to pass out. I'm going to scream. I might *die* if he doesn't stop—

"You are being too rough."

Ezra's voice feels close. I reach out blindly for him, and he grabs my hand and holds it tight. "I am here. You are safe. Let go, Valentina. Come for Mikhail."

The building tension finally snaps, and I crash. My body tightens as every nerve in my body fires off at once, flooding me with endorphins and soothing all my aches and pains. All of the tension in my body melts away as I come back down, relaxing in Mikhail's arms.

He wraps his arms around my middle and holds me tight, *too tight*, hurting my ribs.

"Mikhail, that hurts." I take a shallow breath and grab his wrists. "Hey, it's too tight—"

"You can trust me too, you know." He sighs, resting his forehead against my shoulder. "You don't need Ezra to save you all the time. I'm right here. I'm not going to let anything happen to you."

I open my eyes and blink away tears. *Shit.* Ezra came to my rescue when he thought I was in distress. I mean, I was, but I would have been fine. It's okay if Mikhail pushes my limits. It's okay if *all* of them do. I squeeze Ezra's hand before letting him go.

Ezra stares at me for one long moment before leaving the room.

Finally, Mikhail and I are alone.

"Mikhail, let me go."

He loosens his grip a little, allowing me to turn around and face him. The tub is wide enough that straddling him is easy, and I loop my arms around his neck as I settle into place. He's still rock hard, and it takes strategic maneuvering *not* to sink down onto him.

He won't look at me. But I still catch the stubborn clench of his jaw and the wounded glint in his eye.

I cup his jaw and turn his head towards me. I never would have taken Mikhail for the needy type, but he might be the neediest of my husbands. Ezra's calm and steady. Andrei's confident and clear. But Mikhail—he's turbulent. Arrogant.

And he might not like sharing as much as he lets on.

I run the pad of my thumb across his jawline. "Did you know that the first time Ezra and I met, he didn't say a word to me? At first, I thought he didn't like me." I think back to the hot summer day we met. He'd just been assigned to me, and his first duty as bodyguard was to keep me safe as the women of the family went dress shopping. It was supposed to be an uneventful afternoon.

"But he followed me around all day, as my father ordered. We were walking all around the city that day, from boutique to boutique, for *hours*. It was miserable. My feet were killing me. I stopped watching where I was walking, and I misstepped off the sidewalk and nearly tumbled into the street. But Ezra was watching. He grabbed me right before a taxi sped by. Pulled me back onto the sidewalk before my foot had even touched the ground."

Mikhail's frown deepens, but there's a point I'm trying to make.

"Ezra's always been observant. He can tell when I'm at the edge of something—like danger, or a really fantastic orgasm." I press the tip of my thumb against Mikhail's bottom lip. "He's cautious. He wants to keep me safe before I go past my limits. But *you*, Mikhail, are meant to push those limits." I press my thumb between his lips, past his teeth, and he nips the tip. "I need to expand my safe zone and learn what

I'm capable of—what my body is capable of. I need you, Mikhail. But I don't need you to be safe. I already have a safe man."

He sucks my thumb into his mouth and licks the flat edge, curiosity sparkling in his eyes like flecks of gold. A shiver rolls down my spine, settling between my thighs. His cock twitches, stirring my desire, and I lift my hips to align him to my entrance. Our eyes meet, and I lower myself over the head of his cock. "I need you to be wild, Mikhail. I need you to teach me my limits and help me surpass them." I pull my finger from his mouth to steady myself on his shoulders, getting ready for the drop.

A mischievous smile curves across his lips. "Lesson number one, baby. Sit on my cock."

I lower myself over him slowly, biting my lip as he sinks deeper. But then he flashes that smile, and all of a sudden his hands are on my hips and he *slams* me down, splashing water all around us. I cry out as pleasure zings through me, but Mikhail's already moving, bouncing me on his cock with renewed rigor. He thrusts up to meet me each time I slam back down, punishing me with a promise to deliver exactly what his queen asked for: *something wild.*

I love every gasped breath, every smack of our hips, every splash of water and powerful beat of my heart. The way he grabs my ass *hard*, digging into my flesh to make it hurt, to make me *feel* even more. All of my senses roar at once, over-whelming me.

This is when Ezra would pull me back. My body screams as alarms go off in my head, telling me that this is too much, this is *crazy*, I shouldn't allow him to handle me like this.

But this wild side is still Mikhail. My husband. My lover. I trust him just as much as I trust Andrei and Ezra, and it's time I show him that.

He tosses his head back but keeps his eyes open, watching

me. "Say it again," he hisses, slamming me down. "*Tell me you need me.*"

"I need you!" I wrap my fingers in his hair and tug hard. "I fucking need you, Mikhail. *Yes!* Oh, *yes.*" I lean forward, giving Mikhail complete control and holding on for my life.

My pussy's bruised. My ass is on fire. My knees hurt like a fucking bitch.

But *holyfuckingshit* I'm about to come—

I scream as my walls clench around him, just how he likes, and my body gives in to the pleasure-pain of being thoroughly *fucked*. "I need you," I whine loudly, "I need you so fucking bad, Mikhail, please—"

He grabs my face and crashes our lips together, slamming his cock inside me just in time for his release. He groans into my mouth, pushing his tongue inside as his cock pulses inside my pussy, filling me with his seed.

"I need you, *malyshka*," he murmurs, stroking my cheek. "I need you so fucking bad, it hurts."

I hold him close. I don't know that he's ever been loved before—not like this. Not for who he is, crazy parts and all. "I need you too, Mikhail, so much. I love you."

He exhales slowly, wrapping his arms around my waist and pressing our faces together, cheek to cheek, nose to nose. He kisses my lips, my cheeks, my nose, my forehead, everywhere he can touch. "I love you too, Valentina."

Chapter 18

Valentina

When Andrei tells me that Anton survived the dinner party, at first I'm relieved. One less body to count. One less life on our hands, ratcheting up our tally of victims. Mikhail's the one who tells me about what happened in the wedding chapel —a dozen dead, he says, killed in a sacred space, cowering like trapped animals who know they're about to die.

None of them died with dignity, Ezra tells me. When they were caught, they turned belly-up and begged for their lives.

None were granted mercy.

All the other guests at the wedding lay witness to their screams, their cries, the sounds they made right before they died. I can't imagine the heartbreak. The trauma. But my men see it differently.

"It is Bratva life," Ezra grunts noncommittally, like this is just another day at the office. "They understand this is part of life."

"And business." Andrei straightens his cuffs as he gets ready to leave. We have a meeting with the team who captured Anton after he started raising hell and threatening more lives.

My stomach churns. I don't want to see a reminder of

Liam, and Anton looks strikingly similar to his older brother. But I can't ignore him or let my men handle him for me—I'm part of this Bratva too, even the darkest parts I'm still coming to know.

This is one of those things I'm going to have to get used to.

Mikhail hands me the dress an armed guard delivered to our door. The tag bears Celia's boutique's logo, and the silk flows through my hands like water. It's divine—likely expensive as hell—and definitely hand-picked for me. The deep burgundy pops against my skin, and my mind flashes back to the dinner table.

The poisoned wine staining the tablecloth.

The blood seeping from Liam's body.

The Baranova blood running through *my* veins. Perhaps the Bratva is bathed in blood, both our own and that of our enemies. Maybe that's where the power comes from—what the blood represents. Within these city walls, we have dominion over life itself. We decide who lives and who dies, who is remembered and who is forgotten.

It's a heavy burden for one person to bear. It's no wonder my father became ill and my mother tried to run.

Mikhail zips the back of my dress with a kiss on my shoulder. "You look beautiful, love."

I spin to check the mirror and fix my hair and makeup. I'm not the picture of my mother—all golden and white and pristine. Instead, I am blood and darkness and shadow. The things this Bratva thrives on. The weapons I wield as its queen.

It takes twenty minutes for the four of us to get ready, then another thirty to load into the armored SUV and drive back into the city. I'm nervous about what comes next.

Am I ready to lead this Bratva into its future?

Andrei leans into my side and places a warm hand on my

thigh, kissing my cheek. "Breathe, *zhena*. You were born for this."

We arrive not at the Baranova estate, but at the orphanage. Our car rolls to a stop and my men clamber out of the vehicle double-time, restless for action. We never discussed what to do with Anton. My heart jumps to my throat. Will more blood be shed here, at a place of refuge for displaced children?

I steel my spine as Andrei takes my hand and leads me up the stone walkway. The dark curtains in the window rustle, tiny hands and tiny eyes peering out at us as we approach.

No, this is not a place for bloodshed and manipulation. I need to make sure there are no doubts about this property and these children being off-limits to power plays and violence.

Our children deserve better than that.

The foyer is empty. Francesca is nowhere to be found. I assume if she's one of the seventy-five turncoats, she's already dead. I have little love for the woman, but I know a change in staff will be hard on the kids. Unless, they're used to a revolving door around here as people come and go, in and out of their lives just as quickly as they arrived.

Another grievance against my family for not doing better for these children. Against *me* for abandoning them five years ago.

I won't make that mistake again.

Andrei takes all three of us out back, to a patchwork yard of brown grass and dirt. There are five armored guards, covered head to toe in matching gear, unrecognizable behind their helmets. Then, there's Anton Dolohov.

I'm not used to seeing powerful men on their knees.

One of the guards has his hand on the back of his head, forcing his gaze to the ground. His hands are cuffed behind his back. Two guns are trained on him, while the others scan the perimeter.

It's not a scene a child should witness.

I glance behind us and catch the curtains *whooshing* as children hide from sight. "Who's watching the children?" I frown. If Francesca is missing or dead, did anyone think to assign someone to their care?

Ezra is a master of hiding his emotions, but I'm starting to recognize his tells. His jaw clenches *just* slightly.

That would be a *no one.*

The men may try to reign in their emotions, but I'm not a man, and I'm not about to pretend that this is okay. "Well then. We'll need to make this brief." I drop Andrei's hand and approach Anton on my own. None of my men try to intervene, but Andrei pulls out a handgun from the holster at his hip. I expect him to aim it at Anton in case he tries anything, but instead, he offers it to me.

I stare at the gun for a beat too long.

Andrei places the gun in my hand. "Anton Dolohov needs sentencing." Which translates to, *he needs to die.*

Do they really expect me to kill this man in cold blood, *here?*

I glare at Andrei. He might be okay with shooting Anton in the head and calling it a day, but that's not how I want to run things. "You want him to die." I glance back and Ezra and Mikhail, knowing they expect the same. "You all do."

Mikhail steps up beside me, grabs Anton's blonde head of hair, and wrenches the man's head back. He's been beaten black and blue, his left cheek purpling, his right eye swollen shut. Blood trickles down his nose and from a split lip.

It seems the guards have a few opinions of their own, as well.

"Tell her why you're here, Anton." Mikhail plants his heel on Anton's thigh and digs in, twisting. "Why come to a house full of lonely, desperate kids?"

Anton ignores Mikhail and stares directly at me. "Looks like the pretty girl turned into a beautiful woman overnight.

Tell me, was my brother's cock not enough for you? You had to stuff three cocks in one hole to feel something?"

Mikhail snarls, punching Anton hard in the jaw. The *crack* of knuckles to bone settles in my chest like a heavy stone. I don't feel pity for his pain, but it's the same cycle repeating. We beat someone up. They come back for revenge. We beat someone else up. They return with a gun and a grudge. Over and over and over again.

I'm beginning to understand how the bodies pile up.

Gently, I place my hand on Anton's swollen cheek. He really does look like Liam, even now. "Your brother wanted to own something pretty he could fuck into submission. Do not mistake me for that woman." I tighten my grip, his hot flesh filling my palm as I squeeze. "Answer the question. Why are you here?"

He should have run the first chance he got. It doesn't make sense for him to stay in the city at all. The Dolohovs will be black-listed from ever doing business with the Baranovas again, much less from entering the city.

Anton tries not to react, but a stray tear slips free. It brushes against my finger on its descent to the ground. "The old bitch promised an army. I'm here to collect what we're owed."

My gut twists. Liam and his men had discussed numbers, and Kravinsky even said something about Francesca and the orphanage—the boys not being trained in weaponry. It clicks into place so quickly that I don't notice I'm digging into Anton's face until he screams. Slowly, I pull my nails free, grimacing at the *pluck* from his skin. His blood tips my fingers. I wipe them on his shirt. "What you'll collect is your death."

I draw a breath and let it out slowly. I don't want a man who's willing to abuse children allowed to live. I understand the guards' anger now; anyone who dares touch a child deserves the worst level of hell.

But I am not a dispenser of justice. I will leave that to my men.

Turning to Mikhail, I press a kiss to his cheek. "Make it hurt, *moya muzh.*" I give Andrei his gun back. "Just don't do it here." Finally, I step up to my final husband and place my hand on his chest. "We'll stay here to look after the children for a while." And find Francesca's replacement, and hire a full staff, and make sure all the kids are fed and happy before the day ends. I'd much rather handle these kinds of tasks than the bloody ones.

Leave those to the professionals.

I walk away from Anton and close the door to that part of my life, grateful that it's finally over.

Ezra wrangles the kids and the one remaining staff member into one room while I clean Anton's blood and sweat from my hands. I meant what I said before; these children are under our care, and they deserve better than we've given them. I'm going to make sure they're well taken care of, no matter if they officially join the Bratva or not. That shouldn't be a precursor to their worth.

There are more children and teenagers than I thought. Ezra has a handful of the older ones sitting on two beds as he speaks to them in Russian. A few of them glance in my direction, and I catch the gauntness of their cheeks from across the room. The markings on their necks and arms—brands of the hard life they've been born into. A few of them match Ezra's tattoos.

There's no one better to guide them than him.

A little girl runs over to me and grabs my hand. "Come sit with us!" She pulls me over to a wobbly table and sits with the only two other girls in the room. Plastic cups and mismatched plates sit out in front of all four seats. "We're having tea," the girl explains, "and I've invited the queen!"

I take my seat and smile at each of the girls. I learn their names as Rebecca, their ringleader, fills our cups with water. "My name is Valentina. It's a pleasure to meet you." They ask all kinds of questions about my dress, my hair, the tall man over there, when Miss Francesca will be back, what I'm doing here, when will I be back, and more. It's an endless barrage until we've run out of *tea*, and Rebecca runs off to get more from the sink.

While Ezra and I meet every one of our wards, the staff member pulls all of their records, including all records of employment over the past decade. We'll pour over everything once we're home to determine the best course of action and whether that means fostering children in trusted homes or reworking our current system. Ezra calls in for more staff, and before the sun has set, all children have been fed pork chops and potatoes, watched a movie or played outside, and given new blankets for the night.

It's not perfect, but it's a start.

As Ezra and I make to leave, Rebecca jumps up from her bed and runs out into the hallway. "Queen Valentina!" She rushes into me and hugs my legs tight. "Please come again soon!"

I smooth my hand over Rebecca's hair and crouch to give her a hug. "Of course. I'll bring tea for our party." I lead Rebecca back to bed and tuck her in for the night, then I do the same for the other two girls sharing the room. On our way out, Ezra gives parting words to the older boys in the other rooms.

I take his hand in mine as we walk to the car. "Will you teach me Russian? *Real* Russian, not the little bits and pieces I already know. I want to be able to have full conversations."

"I will do anything for you, *lisichka*." Kissing the back of my hand, he tugs me against his chest. "You look good as mother to them. You have kind heart. They need good influence."

"You seem to be taking to those boys," I point out, lifting an eyebrow. "Maybe fatherhood suits you."

The faintest blush colors Ezra's cheeks, and my heart melts. I push myself onto my tiptoes and kiss him. What begins as a sweet press of lips quickly heats, and he's lifting me into the car and laying me down across the seat within seconds. Our driver closes the door just in time for Ezra to kiss me again, harder, stronger, sighing against my lips as he crawls on top of me.

I look up at my mountain, overwhelmed with emotion. I'm so glad that he's here with me. That he's healing. That he's *mine.*

We don't speak, but we don't have to. We say what we need with gentle caresses and not-so-gentle kisses, coming together in the language we both know works for us. I run my fingers through Ezra's short-cropped hair and sigh as he lifts up my dress to feel me deeper, to claim me as his.

My husband. My guardian. My love.

CHAPTER 19

VALENTINA

OVER THE NEXT FEW DAYS, we spend most of our time reconfiguring our assets and introducing me to the business side of the Bratva. I take Russian lessons from Ezra, political ones from Andrei, and geographical ones from Mikhail. We spend a lot of our time either in Andrei's office, the library, or touring the city in Mikhail's sports car or on Ezra's motorcycle.

But the best part of all comes at the end of a long week, after all of our lessons are complete for the day, and we're able to relax. Andrei leads me out the back of the estate to watch the sunset. We're in the throes of autumn, gearing up for winter, and the leaves around us fall in flurries more each day.

I'm looking forward to cozy nights snuggled between my men, watching the snow fall, or listening to the crackle of a fire.

But for now, enjoying the chill of nightfall and the cascade of fading sunlight feels just as perfect as everything else.

Andrei kisses the top of my head. "I have a surprise for you, *zhena*. Come with me." He takes my hand and brings me past the gardens, across the expanse of withering grass, to the

Baranova cemetery tucked in the back corner of the estate. I haven't been here since Mikhail brought me to my father's grave. There's nothing for me here but a reminder of what's been lost.

My chest aches as we draw near. "I don't want to go in."

If I see my father's plot again, I might be sick. I was so angry when Mikhail showed it to me—when I realized all the lies he'd told and how he hadn't buried my mother like he'd promised.

If Andrei is taking me to see my grandmother's plot, I might *really* get sick. She is no better than my father, in the end. "I thought we weren't burying her." I keep my gaze unfocused as I'm brought to the center of the cemetery, where my father's been buried. I don't want to see it. I don't want to feel all the hurt and anger and resentment after spending so many days healing, surrounded by love.

All I'll find here is heartbreak and grief.

"I don't want to be here, Andrei."

He glances at me from over his shoulder. "Do you trust me?"

I take a deep breath. Of course I trust him. I follow him deeper into the cemetery. At first, I keep my eyes on the fading pinks and purples in the sky, avoiding the inevitable end of our journey, and the emotions I'll have to face. I know, he's probably wanting to give me closure.

But I don't want it.

I could never come back here again and be okay with that.

It isn't until we've come to a stop that I finally lower my gaze.

I don't understand what I'm looking at. Two trees frame a simple, white stone lying flat in the earth. My father's tall, domineering tombstone is missing—in fact, all of the dirt and decay surrounding it is gone. In its place are seasonal flowers delicately composed around the new memorial and a stone path leading to it.

"You redid my father's grave?" The dirt's been disturbed, chopped up to put in the flowers and decor. It's *pretty*.

Nothing about my father was, or should be, pretty.

Andrei shakes his head. "I thought we could put something better here." Gently, he pulls me beneath the canopy and onto the path. I stare at the new white granite headstone, squinting to read the etching in the fading light.

In memory of Maeve Baranova, beloved mother and protector

Tears fill my eyes. "Mom?" I lower myself to my knees and brush my fingertips over the stone. She will finally be honored in the way she deserves. It's not enough to make up for the past, but it's close.

Andrei squeezes my hand as he kneels by my side. "Mikhail told me what happened when he brought you here before. I had your father removed from the property and this built in its place. We'll replace the flowers each season so that there is always something in bloom, and the trees will grow to encompass a much larger space, in time. They should bloom in the spring with pink flowers. We can add a bench, if you'd like, or a fountain. Whatever you think Maeve would like, or what you would like. This is a space for the two of you."

I can't stop the tears from coming. They flow freely, wetting my cheeks and blurring my vision. I swipe at my eyes, but it's no use. I'm overflowing with love—for my mother, for Andrei, for this space he's given us. "Thank you," I murmur, holding in a sob. "Thank you so much."

He pulls me into his chest and lets me cry against him. My tears turn into sobs, wracking my body. I wish my mom were here for real, to see the love I share with these men. To see what we're going to build together. How we're going to reshape the Bratva to be better than she experienced.

I'll carry her with me in memory, and I'll come here to share pieces of my life with her. I glance around the cemetery at all the graves. Maybe we can spruce the entire place up. Expand the gardens to encompass the family cemetery. Make it a place of remembrance instead of one of death.

The sun sets with an indigo haze overhead, and amber-colored solar lights flick on, hanging from the two trees and lighting the path back home. We stay for a while longer while I tell Andrei stories about my mother: who she was, how she loved, and which parts of her I see reflected within me.

～

Two Months Later

Snow blankets the ground in a sheet of white, undisturbed if it weren't for my trek to my mother's memorial. Andrei insists on having our groundskeepers shovel the snow, but I like how quiet everything is in the winter. The whole world stills, waiting on bated breath for the first stirrings of spring.

I can't believe how quickly time has flown by, nor can I believe how much has changed in a few short months. I'm more fluent in Russian thanks to Ezra's tutelage, and I can navigate the entire city without relying on a GPS. Andrei has introduced me to every prominent member of society that we're on good terms with, and the children's home is flourishing with its new headmistress and foster program in full swing.

I couldn't have done any of it alone. And now, especially, I'll need more help than ever.

I lay out the waterproof blanket I brought with me, then sit in the middle of my mother's grove. I lay a second, thick wool blanket over my legs and wrap my cloak tighter around me. My breaths puff into the air and crystallize in the freezing temperatures. I won't be able to stay out here too long, but there's something I need to confess.

I lace my fingers together in my lap. "I think I might be pregnant." I've felt different lately. Cramping at random moments. A little irrational with my emotions. "I haven't taken a test or anything, and I haven't told my husbands. I'm not sure what they'll say."

Andrei wants at least one child, maybe more. He says he's okay with adopting, but I know he'd love one of his creation. Mikhail plays indifferent, but he's become obsessed with filling me with his cum and keeping his cock buried inside for as long as possible. I know it's because he's trying to get me pregnant. And Ezra . . . he's the one with that unmistakable glimmer of hope in his eyes. He does well with the kids at the orphanage, but I catch him watching me interact with the children more and more as time goes on.

They all want hope for our future.

But I don't know if I'm ready for it.

"Were you ready to be a mom?" I listen for any sign that she's here with me. A bird chirps nearby, and I imagine that it's her. "I know that you married young and that your main purpose was producing an heir." I bite my lip. It's the same role I was meant to play, in the before. Things are different now, and I have an active role in decisions involving the Bratva and its people. But does that mean that I can have a baby girl and everything will still be okay?

"I don't know how to tell them."

I guess I should take a test first. But they'll know if I go out and buy one.

My phone buzzes in my pocket, and I pull it out to find a text from Celia about a gala she's attending soon, asking if I'm going. I quickly type a message before I lose my nerve.

> Can I come over?

Her reply is an immediate *yes*, and I breathe a sigh of relief. If anyone can keep a secret, it's Celia. The woman's been keeping many of her own, lately.

I get Ezra to drop me off in her driveway an hour later. He unclasps my helmet and gives me a tender kiss. "Let me know when ready for pick up." His phone chimes, and we both already know who it is.

Mikhail's been agitated that his sister won't return his calls. He likely received a GPS ping once we arrived at her house.

"He is stubborn bastard," Ezra sighs. "I will handle him. Enjoy visit, *lisichka*." We kiss a little longer before I walk to the front door. Once Celia opens it with a wave, he drives off into the distance.

Celia ushers me inside, and the first thing I notice is that her home feels more lived-in than before. The blanket on the couch isn't folded, the candles around the house have all been burned to the ends, and there are handprints on some of her walls that you can see in the right slant of light. I raise an eyebrow at a bottle of lube I spy on her coffee table.

She clears her throat and shoves the bottle into a random drawer. "Excuse the mess. I've had company."

"I can see," I muse, trying to hide my smile but failing. "It must be really good company if you left the lube out." I laugh as she blushes crimson, like I've caught her in a scandal. "I'm not judging, I promise! I'm happy for you!"

Celia sucks her cheeks in. "Thank you. It's all very new. I'm still adjusting to things." She brushes chestnut hair over her shoulder, revealing a love bite she may not realize is there. "But *that* conversation calls for wine. White or red, Val?" She slips into the kitchen and pops open her wine cooler.

"None for me, thanks."

Her hand freezes on the door, and she turns to face me in slow motion. "Are you sure? I've got a peach flavor that's to die for." She smiles, but it's pinched at the edges. "Too early for a drink?"

I clear my throat. "I actually wanted your help with something. I know it's rude to come over and ask for a favor, but—"

She shakes her head, shutting the wine cooler and coming over to take both my hands in hers. "Never apologize. We're sisters, Valentina. What do you need?"

Her warm chocolate eyes bore into mine. When we first met, I thought she was a spitting image of her brother, but her eyes are a shade lighter, and a few freckles dust her cheeks, whereas Mikhail has none. Taking a breath, I ask for the secret favor. "Please don't tell them, but I think I might be pregnant. Do you have a test I could use?"

Her eyes tear up a little, and she nods. "Of course, honey." She swipes her eyes, a tiny laugh spilling past her lips. "Oh, look at me. I'm such a mess. Sorry about the tears." She takes a quick breath. "I have plenty of tests, Valentina. Take as many as you'd like, then you can take some home, too, okay?"

I squeeze her hands in mine. "Are you okay?"

She smiles, sweeter this time. "I've never been better. I promise."

We head upstairs to her master bath and she shows me a full drawer of pregnancy tests. Some are little pink strips, while others are the plastic sticks you pee on, still wrapped in the box. Celia lets me pick which ones I want. "When Caleb and I were trying, I got a little carried away. But! We don't want these to go to waste, now, do we? Take as many as you'd like."

"I don't need all of them." I grab five and leave about ten more in the drawer. "I can take two here, then bring three home. One for each of my men to see." I nearly roll my eyes at the thought that each man needs his own test to prove I'm pregnant or not, but I wouldn't put it past them.

Especially Mikhail.

"Well, if you need more, you know where to find them."

I thank Celia as she closes the door on her way out. Then, I spend a few minutes reading the instructions on the box. I already know what to do; I'm merely stalling for time. Taking a deep breath, I sit on the toilet and will myself to pee.

Taking a test shouldn't be this hard.

As I wait for the results of test number one, I take test number two, then clean up and sit on the edge of the tub.

All that's left to do now is wait.

Celia knocks gently. "Everything okay in there?"

"Just waiting."

"Do you want some company?"

I open the door and let Celia inside. She perches on the vanity while we wait. "You know," she says after a pregnant pause, "it's okay to be nervous. Having a baby is a big change, and you've gone through a lot of change lately." She rubs my shoulder fondly. "No one will blame you for being unsure about what comes next."

I take a deep breath and hold it. I can picture Ezra cradling the tiniest little baby in his arms, gently rocking it to sleep. Or Mikhail, bringing her a thousand stuffed toys and footie pajamas that she'll have to grow into. Andrei napping on the couch with the baby swaddled against his chest. All of these little fragments are wishes for the future.

I *do* want a baby. *So* much. That's what scares me—that

this is all in my head, or that I'll lose the baby before it's even born, or that I'll somehow mess her up with my genes. "I come from a pretty messed up family," I admit slowly. "I didn't realize it until I got older, but. . . things weren't as perfect as they seemed." I think of my beautiful mother and all the secrets hidden behind her smiles. "I don't know if my parents really loved each other."

It makes me sad to think that my mother never knew what it felt like to be loved. Sure, Katya must have loved her daughter, but the touch of a lover who's *in love* with you feels wonderful. It's like sunlight kissing your skin after a cold winter's night—warm and glowing and full of life.

"Then there's the whole *Baranova* thing, with my bloodline. It's made me a target." I wrap my arms around my stomach. "I've been a bargaining chip my whole life. I don't want that to happen to my baby." My biggest fear is that they'll go through the same things I did and be just as naïve and manipulated as I was. "What if I can't protect them? What if having my blood is a curse?"

Celia hops off the vanity and buries me in a hug. "*If* you're pregnant," she begins softly, "then your baby is lucky to have a mother who cares so much. And her fathers?" She huffs a quick laugh. "They'll be so in love with her because she's a part of *you*, and they love their momma fiercely. They love *themselves* too. Mainly Mikhail, so he'll double-love her for being a mini version of himself." That makes us both chuckle. "But she'll also have an auntie who won't let a damned thing happen to her." Celia winks. "She'll be popular in the city as a Baranova, yes, but that also means that the Bratva will look after her. You'll see."

"*If* I'm pregnant."

She squeezes my hand. "Let's find out."

I swallow and stare at the two plastic sticks sitting on the back of the toilet. I pick them up at the same time and slowly turn them over, my heart racing.

Two pink lines confirm it.

I'm pregnant.

Now, I have to tell the fathers.

Chapter 20

Valentina

The drive home feels faster than ever before, and I know Ezra took the scenic route to spend more time with me. It doesn't matter that all we did was drive around on the back of his motorcycle; it still counts as *us* time. The scenery is usually beautiful around the park and along the coastline, but my heart isn't in it today.

Ezra must notice because I'm not gripping him as hard on the turns as I usually do. I'm lost in thought, worrying about the three tests crammed in my bra. I know they'll all turn up positive.

I just don't know what I'll do if any of my men *aren't* happy about it.

We come to a stop at the estate garage, and Ezra kicks off the engine. I don't want to move yet, so I hold him tight and bury my face in his back. He pauses after taking off his helmet. "What is wrong, *lisichka*? Are you frozen?"

I'm actually *very* warm, thanks to Ezra's insane body heat.

"No." I pry myself loose. "Thank you for bringing me home."

He helps me off the bike and takes off my helmet.

Cupping my face in his hands, he leans in and presses a kiss to my forehead. "How was visit?"

"It was good. Celia's wonderful, like always."

He studies my face. "Mikhail is worrying. He will ask about visit."

"I know, he's annoyed that she won't talk to him." I haven't asked Celia what's up, but I know Mikhail wants answers for her sudden silence. I won't have them. "I'm trying to stay out of it."

Ezra half-shrugs. "I do not have sibling to understand situation. But I have feeling it is about chapel incident. She will get over it, in time."

"And if she doesn't?"

"Then we will have broken twin on hands, hm?"

My stomach clenches. I sometimes forget that Mikhail and Celia are twins. "Does that run in the family? Twins?"

Could I be pregnant with twins right now?

Ezra grunts, a noncommittal answer. "I do not know." His eyes narrow as I avoid his gaze. I fear he'll see right through me, straight to the pregnancy tests shoved inside my bra. "Why do you ask?"

"N-no reason." I pull away from him and make a speedy retreat for the door. "Where are the others?"

"Valentina." Ezra crosses his arms over his broad chest. "Why are you asking about twins?" His tone sharpens as I ignore his question. "*Valentina.*"

I don't know what to say without blurting out *I'm pregnant!* If I open my mouth, the words will come tumbling out, and I *can't.* I can't tell one of them without telling the others.

He catches up to me lightning-fast, grabbing my wrist and forcing me to stop fleeing. "I asked question. I would like answer." After a moment, he sighs. "Please."

My heart pounds fast and hard, like how Ezra pounded me this morning when he came inside me. Or like Mikhail, just yesterday on the dining room table. Or Andrei, the evening before, bent over his desk like a cheap whore as he lifted up my thigh and *railed* me. They've been ravenous, filling me up every chance they get. Not that I'm complaining—I have more dick than I have sense, right now.

I'm two weeks late for my period, too. If they haven't noticed that by now, someone's bound to sniff it out sooner or later.

I bite my bottom lip. Do I tell him? Or do I try to hold out another five minutes until we're all together?

His nostrils flare, and he backs me against the wall. "Do you have secret for us, *moya zhena*?" My knees buckle at the phrase. He knows I love being called their wife.

I keep my mouth shut, but his eyes light up like he's just been given the most precious gift in the world. *My secret.* Our secret. *Our truth.* He pins me to the wall, lifting my arms over my head and sighing against my lips. "You smell like honey, sweet to taste. I want to make love to sweet wife." He cups my jaw, tilting my head back and tasting my lips. I whimper and claw at his shoulders.

God, just being around him turns me on.

He nips the shell of my ear, breathing hard. "But she must tell secret first." His hands find my breasts and squeeze.

Then he stops moving.

Shit. The tests. He feels the tests.

He pulls back and stares at my boobs. "What are you hiding, Valentina?" A frown etches across his face. "If it is drugs, I will help you get clean."

"No! No, it's not that!" I cover my boobs with my hands. I know he can't see anything through my shirt, but it makes me feel like I can hold the truth in a little longer. "I need to talk to you guys. Now. Please. Can we go inside?"

Ezra presses his lips together in a thin line. "Okay. We go inside, then you tell secret."

He follows me inside the house, staying silent as we make our way to the master bedroom. Since the four of us started sleeping together, Andrei added a second king-sized mattress to the room, pressed up against the first. We use my room down the hall for storing clothes and our favorite sets of guns and knives.

Our master suite is mainly used for sex, sleep, and showers.

When we walk into the room, Andrei looks up from the book he's reading in his favorite armchair. "Welcome back. Did you have fun?"

Before I can answer, Mikhail bursts from the bathroom with a towel wrapped around his waist, his hair dark and dripping wet from his shower. He sighs dramatically. "Finally, you're back. Did you see anything suspicious? Did she say anything about me?"

Ezra places his palm on my lower back, keeping me moving toward my other two husbands. "Valentina has something in breast pocket."

Some of the annoyance in Mikhail's gait melts away. "Oooh, did you steal something, love?" He grabs my waist and brings me in for a lingering kiss. "I like it when you do bad things." He slides his palm beneath my shirt and up my stomach to cup my breasts. He gives them a hard squeeze, curiosity flickering in his eyes. "Can I see?"

I nod, and he lifts my shirt over my head. Ezra undoes the bra clasp at my back, and I pull off my bra. It falls to the floor, and Mikhail catches the pregnancy tests in his hands. His eyes widen. "Are these—have you—?"

Andrei snaps his book shut and drops it into his chair. "Show me, Mikhail."

He tosses one of the tests into Andrei's chest, then drops the other two to the floor. "Your period is late." His smile is sweet one second, then wicked the next. "I've been filling your pussy up good, haven't I?" He palms my stomach with one hand, then my ass with the other. "Keeping my cock inside you as long as possible. Making sure my cum gets nice and deep."

Ezra sighs at my back. "Mikhail, you are not only man sleeping with her."

"There are three of us," Andrei comments, smacking the pregnancy test against his open palm. "That's a sixty-six percent chance that you're not the father."

I look between the three of them, shaking my head. "You can't seriously be territorial about this baby. It's *ours*, no matter which one of you is the father."

Andrei's head snaps back in my direction. "So you *have* taken a test."

"Take another," Mikhail insists, grabbing the one from Andrei's hand and placing it into mine. "I'll come with you."

"She does not need help to pee," Ezra grumbles, wrapping his arms around me from behind. He gently palms my stomach, like he's protecting me from the others.

Or keeping me and the baby to himself.

Mikhail scoffs. "Of course she does. She'll need help with everything now. We have to make sure she and the baby stay safe throughout the entire pregnancy."

I take as deep of a breath as I can, but it's painfully shallow. My heart flutters in my chest like it's about to leap out from my ribs and fly far, far away. "Guys," I whisper, blinking rapidly. They're looking a little fuzzy at the edges.

They continue arguing over the stupidest things.

"*Guys.* I think I need to lie down."

All three of them shut up immediately, and Ezra lifts me into his arms like I weigh nothing. He carries me to the bed and lays me down gently, like I'm made of glass. Andrei removes my shoes, then my pants and panties, before tucking me beneath the covers. Mikhail's towel has disappeared in the time it took for him to reach the bed, and he slips in beside me. "I'm sorry, baby, I got carried away. Are you okay?" He brushes curls behind my ear.

They all stare at me with concern in their eyes.

"You're going to have to get along better." You'd think after years of working together, they would have figured out how to keep the peace between themselves. "Or you'll stress me and the baby out."

"Of course. We will." Andrei gives both Ezra and Mikhail a withering look. "Right, brother?"

They both nod. Ezra kisses the back of my hand, while Mikhail nuzzles against my cheek. "We'll do anything you say, Valentina. Whatever you need."

I stretch my legs with a sigh. Having Mikhail curled against my side is nice, but I have two other men I'd *also* like to cuddle. "Get in bed. All of you. I want to touch my husbands."

Ezra crawls into bed behind me and lays my head in his lap. Mikhail stays curled up on one side, and Andrei takes the other. All three of them take turns caressing my stomach, my thighs, my breasts, kissing my body all over. It's enough to make a girl burn with need, but my eyes flutter closed more than once.

"Get some sleep," Andrei orders, turning my face towards him to kiss my lips. "We're not going anywhere."

Mikhail kisses me next, sucking my bottom lip between his, a groan catching in the back of his throat. "You're so fucking sexy, Valentina. I promise to fuck you hard when you wake up." He purrs in my ear. "Or while you sleep. Whichever you want, baby."

"You will *not* fuck her in sleep."

A giggle passes my lips. "Maybe some gentle sex during my nap is okay."

"Be careful what wish for," Ezra grunts, his cock already

hardening next to my ear. "Because we will deliver on promise, *zhena.*"

"*Moya prekrasnaya zhena,*" Andrei murmurs, sliding his hand between my thighs. He teases my clit with light brushes of his fingertips, making me sigh with pleasure. "Sleep. We'll take good care of you and the baby."

"We always will."

I grab Mikhail and Andrei's hands and hold them to my chest, a smile on my lips.

I know my men will keep their promise.

I couldn't ask for better fathers for our beautiful baby girl.

Epilogue

Mikhail

It's been weeks since I've heard from my sister.

It's not like her to ignore me for so long, but then again, it's not like her to be mad at me for this long, either. We've had our little disagreements over the years, but this one was huge. She won't forgive me for a long time.

But this silent treatment bullshit has got to end. I'm going to be a *father*, for crying out loud. I'd like to celebrate that with my twin sister *before* the baby pops out.

I pound my fist against Celia's front door. "Celia, open up! You can't be mad at me forever!" I back up to glance at her garage door, noting her car parked inside, then go right back to her front porch. "I know you're in there!"

Movement from behind the door catches my attention, and I breathe a sigh of relief. *Thank God* she has some sense. I really didn't want to have to break down her door to see her.

She'd hate me a little for that, too.

The door unlocks, and I'm already trying to step across the threshold when I'm stopped by someone who is *not* my sister. A man blocks my path. A man who looks familiar, but whose name I can't place. Dark hair sweeps across his forehead, and the cocky smile on his face makes me want to punch the fucker. "Celia's tied up at the moment. Can I take a message?"

"Get out of my way." I try to shove past the man, but he blocks my entry with an arm on the doorjamb and a grin that pisses me off. "Don't make me stab you," I hiss, pulling my knife from its hidden sheath and pressing it against his abdomen. "Because I'll make it hurt."

"The famous Mikhail Monrovia, stab *me*?" He flourishes his hand against his chest. "I'm honored. Go ahead."

The fucker's crazy, but so am I.

I press the knife deeper, cutting through his stupid v-neck shirt—what fucking adult *wears* those—and shove the tip into his gut. It shouldn't hit anything important here, but if he rams it deeper, he'll be hurting.

The man hisses, dark eyes alight with joy. "You're going easy on me, Monrovia. I said, *stab me*."

Fine.

The knife goes deep, three solid inches, through the muscle and into his body cavity. I've been stabbed before—that shit fucking *hurts*. But this man starts *laughing*, running his hand through his hair as he cackles. "Fuck, man, I love it. I'll tell your sister you send your regards." He claps his hand on my shoulder. "Welcome to the family, Monrovia. Glad to have you."

He backs up, unsticking the knife, and moves to close the door.

I block it with my foot and shove it open as wide as I can. Behind this man is another—a larger, taller one, who's a damn near spitting image of the first one.

Brothers.

Russian brothers, by the looks of their tattoos. I only spot two, but I know there's a third—the worst one of all—and then the *fourth* half-brother just waltzed back into the Bratva on a golden fucking pardon granted by Andrei Leonov himself. I knew it wasn't a good idea to let him back in. Now, his brothers are terrorizing *my* sister, because they think they can.

I curse aloud. *Fuck,* they shouldn't be here. I glare at both of them. What the hell are their names? Ezra told me once. Twice. I can never remember. They're not traditional ones; they go by some made-up shit.

Valentina would know. She keeps up with these things. I know real estate and property ownership—I don't know our members as well.

"This is Baranova property—and I'm ordering you to get the hell out." I fight against the stabbed one to push open the door. He's stronger than me, even while injured. I should have twisted the knife when I had the chance.

The taller brother steps closer, not nearly as amused as the other one. "This house is under our protection now, Monrovia. I suggest you stand down before someone gets hurt. I'd hate to tell Celia that we broke her brother's arm for putting his nose where it doesn't belong."

I grit my teeth. "You wouldn't dare. I'm your boss."

He shrugs. "Ezra is our boss. Take it up with him."

They shut the door in my face, leaving me fuming on the doorstep. I rattle the handle, to no use. All the curtains are closed. The lights are on upstairs, and I catch shadows moving around the room. She's got to be up there with one of them.

I speed-dial Ezra immediately. "Get your men out of my sister's house," I hiss, "before I gun them down."

Ezra sighs. "What is wrong?"

"She's been—I don't know, kidnapped!"

"In her own home?"

"Yes! Your fucking guys are in there—the brothers. The ones with the names. I want them out."

Ezra is silent for a moment. "Has your sister contacted you?"

I pace across her driveway. No, she hasn't contacted me. Not since the botched wedding. She was furious with me for what happened. What I *allowed* to happen.

She doesn't understand Bratva business. We had traitors among us; they couldn't be allowed to live another moment, or the infection could have spread and made things much, much worse.

"No. She won't return my calls." I've watched her work through her boutique windows, but I haven't gone inside. "I know she's safe because she's been working. But they're in there, Ezra, doing God knows what to her!"

Ezra chuffs. "You know what they are doing."

I keep the mental image as PG as possible. "She wants a family, Ezra, not three—or four—psychopaths."

"They can be family, too."

I roll my eyes. "Please. The day Celia gives up her picture-perfect life for anything remotely resembling *those three*, I'll go insane."

"What do you think is happening now, Mikhail?"

With a growl, I hang up the phone. Ezra is of no help. I march back up the two little porch steps and—the big one is watching me through the curtains. *Fuck me.*

I take a deep breath and try to think things through. Where did she even meet them? It's not like she crosses paths with the Bratva regularly. They're not her cookie-cutter clientele. She wouldn't be caught dead with them in public.

A lightbulb goes off, and I absolutely fucking hate it.

She wouldn't be seen with them in public, so where would they have met?

The brothers run that fucking sex club.

The only way in is through direct invitation.

They saw her at Andrei and Valentina's second wedding. They saw her defend all those people with nothing but her fury and her fists. It's a kind of determination that my sister normally keeps locked up tight until that exact moment she needs it. At the chapel, she needed it to protect complete strangers from annihilation.

She let her inner fire burn bright, and it caught the attention of three demons.

I run a hand down my face. I don't like it. They're not safe men to be around. They'll hurt her to wring their pleasure from her in any way they can. But I've seen them in action; they helped rescue Valentina from the late mayor's mansion, and they've worked with Ezra on dozens of retrieval and removal missions. He trusts them with his life.

Now, they're asking me to trust my sister's life with them. No. *Demanding* it.

But what if that's what Celia wants?

I glare at the window one last time before turning around and heading back to my car. I'll ask Celia herself about it instead of speculating on her behalf. For now, I know she's at least well-guarded, if not *safe* in the firmest sense of the word.

That will have to be enough.

CELIA'S STORY ISN'T OVER

Three brothers claim the one woman they've vowed to make their wife. One night of passion binds her to them forever.

Read the beginning of Celia's reverse harem romance in my free novella *Brutal Beauty*.

Preorder Celia's full length book, *Beautiful Rage*, on my website.

Why should I preorder on your website instead of on my favorite retailer? To be 100% transparent, purchasing books on my website ensures that more of your investment comes directly to me, and money is received within days instead of months later, upon the book's release. Your contribution is what makes character art, alternate covers, professional editing, book boxes, etc. possible. Thank you for your support. It means the absolute world to me. 🩶

Want more of the Baranova Bratva?
Join my newsletter for exclusive bonus scenes (coming soon!).

Russian Terminology

Throughout the book, various Russian words and phrases are referenced. Here are their definitions.

Babushka: *grandmother*
Da: *yes*
Durak: *fool*
Pakhan: *leader of the Russian bratva*
Lisichka: *little fox*
Malyshka: *little girl or baby girl*
Moye ditya: *my child*
Moya prekrasnaya zhena: *my beautiful wife*
Moya zhena: *my wife*
Mudak: *Bastard/Asshole*
Muzh: *Husband*
Nyet: *No*
Shlyukha: *whore*
Suka: *bitch*
Vors: *captains*
Zhena: *wife*

Acknowledgments

Valentina's family means a lot more to me now than I could have ever imagined.

When I first conceptualized Valentina over a year ago, I wanted her to be a strong-willed woman (a med student, actually) who would reshape the Bratva with a kind heart and gentle soul. I intended for fate to guide her back to the Bratva after she suffered memory loss, and for her men to find her and bring her home.

As you can see, her story changed significantly, and so did her men.

In the first draft of *Rule of Three*, something was missing. Valentina was meant to be queen, but she kept allowing men to choose her path. She was reactionary instead of creating change and taking charge of her own life.

Her journey from Princess to Queen couldn't happen simply because she married a man. That's not the story I wanted to tell.

She needed to go through a transformation. She needed to dig deep and overcome the challenges in front of her on her own —not to rely on Prince Charming to save her.

I like to think that the current version of Valentina is stronger not only because of what she has overcome, but because of the men who lift her up and encourage her to shine bright, no matter if it's in the sharpest daylight or darkest night. She is beautiful in all capacities, and she is strong enough to handle anything.

Her men are there to pick her up when she falters, and that's okay. It's okay to need help. It's okay to *admit* you need help, too.

Our big boy Ezra struggles with the weight of protecting his family, but he never complains, even when he goes beyond his limits to ensure their safety. The selflessness he shows is something that I find many of us who are *givers* tend to embody. It's wonderful to love your friends and family and put them first, but you have to take care of yourself, too. I hope that if you're reading this and you're someone who gives so much of yourself that there is little left for *you*, that you remember to safeguard your own health and well-being. Your loved ones will thank you for protecting yourself, too.

Our first love Andrei wants a family *so bad*. His own parents disappeared when he was young—the only constant in his life has been Ezra. . . until Valentina arrives. Her departure cut him deep, but her return helped sooth the scars over his heart. The fact that she chose to stay with him is what makes him love her that much harder. (Not that he would have let her walk away again. 😢)

Mikhail, oh, Mikhail. The man who wants nothing more than to have something to treasure. Something precious, more valuable than riches or fame or beauty. The man who has *everything* except the one thing he wants. When he first meets Valentina, he knows he desires her. But he doesn't realize just how precious she will become. As he catches glimmers of her true self, he starts to wonder . . . will she want him back? The bathtub scene in *Reign of Four* happened organically; it was unplanned, and the words flew from my fingertips. I wasn't sure where the story was going, but when it was complete, I knew it was Mikhail's moment of vulnerability. Valentina needed to reassure him that she loved him just as he was. She will always be his precious treasure.

All of these characters are important to me, and I hope that you've enjoyed their story. But it's only the beginning—we're not leaving the Baranova Bratva *just* yet. Stick around for extra scenes between our main family, and then have a taste of *Midnight* with Celia Monrovia, as she unravels her perfect life one thread at a time.

A huge, unending thank you goes to so many people. My beta readers, my good friend Angel, my husband, my dogs, the Universe. Every time I slip into self-doubt about my writing, or my goals of becoming a full-time author seem unattainable or foolish, someone comes along and reminds me that *I got this*. Whether it's a kind word about my writing, or my tenacity, or full-blown support, it appears right when I need it.

Thank you from the bottom of my heart. I couldn't do this without all of the people lifting me toward my dreams. 🖤

ABOUT THE AUTHOR

Just a smut-lover listening to angsty love songs on repeat.

Misti Wilds loves watching characters pine after one another from afar--until a tall, dark, brooding alpha male says *fuck this* and claims his woman. But one man isn't enough these days--Misti's got her hands full when it comes to writing multiple dark and delicious men with violence in their hearts and a declaration of love etched on the barrel of their guns.

Why choose one when you can have them all?

ALSO BY MISTI WILDS

Baranova Bratva:

Rule of Three

Reign of Four

Brutal Beauty

Claimed by Rage

Tempted to Rebel

Bound by Ruin

Broken Vows

Made in the USA
Middletown, DE
30 August 2024